THE GARDEN

THE GARDEN

by

Yves Berger

Translated from the French by

Robert Baldick

George Braziller
New York

129376

For Jean Paulhan,

    the PATRON

But at my back I always hear
Time's winged chariot hurrying near.

> —MARVELL
> *To his Coy Mistress*

With steam-engines and electricity, the world's
insomnia began.

> —GUGLIELMO FERRERO
> *Speech to the Deaf*

You are not an American with an Indian's broad
shoulders and slim waist, with level eyes and a skin
tanned by the air of the prairies and the rivers that
cross them, you have not been to the Great Lakes and
sailed on them, wherever they may be. So, I ask you,
what would a pretty girl like me be doing following
you?

> —FRANZ KAFKA
> *Contemplation*

THE GARDEN

DURING the day, it would be an understatement to say that I think about nothing, that I am like an automaton, giving orders to this person and that and attending to things here and there; the fact is that during the day it is as if I were not alive. I am neither hungry nor thirsty, and I sit down to table out of habit. I am superior to you in this respect: time. It affects and governs the world, but over me it has no power, on me it has no effect. It is rather I who command it: Come along, time, we are going to sit down to table. Time sits down with me. Then we forget each other.

My relations with time would make my father, if he came back, secretly happy. I say "secretly" because he would not show anything. It took more than satisfaction and even more than joy to make him abandon his reserve. It took torments, passions. And I remember only one occasion when he was really carried away by emotion, and that emotion finally carried him off.

My relations with time may make my sister, if she ever returns, rather concerned. She will say that I am turning out like father. But that is not true, I am not turning out like anything or anybody, and of this immobility I have a proof: time.

It is at night that my life begins. Again, then, I think of my father and how he would be happy, secretly, to know that I am dedicated to the stars. I tell myself that he must have loved them, toward the end of his life, because they never moved, never changed, stronger than the moon—which the clouds can always cut up—or the sun, which takes on different colors. He must have dreamed, in his last moments, of hanging himself on a star.

I have changed nothing in the ordering of his house, in the arrangement of his garden. It is into my father's garden that I go in the evening, together with the first stars, in my father's garden that I sit down, in his place on the green bench, right against the lime tree, which he liked to feel beside him and, if he was speaking, to touch. Not that I spend hours there, any more than elsewhere during the day. The stars disappear and I go in to sleep. The workmen have no need of me, I gave them their orders yesterday, last year, ten years ago, an eternity ago.

I never knew the time—and already, in my father's day, it was the end, which he wanted to delay—when, once the herds had been brought in, once the smell of sheep, wool and grease had been absorbed, the night belonged to silence, to vagabond scents, and when it rose, to the wind alone, whose breath no one would have dared to take away. I grew up in the midst of noise and gasoline. My life is ravaged by the laughter of the men and youths who go to the village, into the square where the five cafés and the brothel are. All the same, my father, Virginie my sister, and others too, chose the night for me, and, in the garden, this place on the bench. Their obstinacy repairs the web in which they have imprisoned me. When the laughter dies away, it is as if it had never been.

In my memories, my mother is confused with the maidservant. Virginie has gone.

I can hear my father saying: "Come back, little nanny goat." He had read everything.

We know that he died because the mare was galloping along at breakneck speed, bolting perhaps. Some people added that a car, several cars were not keeping to the right. That may well be so. But it is not true, as people said on hearing about the accident, that my father, for some time past, had been a different man. And those who push back the moment when he changed, as if they had been close acquaintances, shrewd, knowing folk, they too deceive themselves, out of complacency and a taste for gossip. My father has always been my father. With me, before me.

I had a presentiment of his death. I came back to the village, to the house, for his sake, not to take his place, but to succeed him. All that time I spent at school, close to Virginie, far from my father, must not be given a significance which I know it did not have. My failure with my sister and that frenzied writing work which I undertook at that time, insane as I was under Virginie's influence, are things of no importance, such as happen to everybody, which reveal nothing, prove nothing. If they recounted my story, those who have heard it, or if I for my part let myself go, I know there would be people who would draw a moral from it. People with imagination. Pretentious people, mythmakers. There is nothing to get out of a dead past, a failure,

4

a ruin. My life is with my father, dead, alive, in the garden where every day the dying day gives place once more to the uninterrupted night. The official from the *Mairie* found me there at that time. I had to go back into the house, look for some papers, read them, then sign at the bottom of a page which he held out to me, under a date.

A date! So it was two years ago that I came home. In the morning my arrival, the accident in the evening. Yes. But I can see once more the group at the garden gate, young men, bronzed or copper-colored, whom the villagers called niggers, my father Indians. How can I have forgotten that number, 1956, which is something like a date of birth since there is nothing, in the night or the garden or my life, which does not emanate from it, and when I say my life I mean that slow mixing-up of a past, that recapitulation of violent episodes and thoughts, that fervor driving on my brain which is as compact as the earth, so that one and the same rotation, every night, brings us both back, the earth and me, to this fixed point: my father. Those men were Italians, Spaniards. A score of them around his body, which two of them were holding by the shoulders and the knees. I have been told what happened after the accident: my father was put inside a car. The road was obstructed:

5

those foreigners, walking at their ordinary pace, stayed around him. At the entrance to the village the driver parked his car: he knew my father. The local people, standing on their doorsteps, in their street, watched the procession. They did not move. The men at the head of the cortege knew instinctively that the dead man's house was ours, where no one was waiting. I can understand the villagers. They were too astonished to accept that twist of fate: my father escorted by men whose recruitment, from outside the country, he disapproved of, in spite of the disappearance of the local day laborers. Bringing in the wine harvest was something we should do ourselves. I think too that their attitude now was intolerable. The men had been available immediately . . . and sooner than anyone else. Their concern, their kindliness, their competence deprived the villagers of a duty which should have fallen to them and of the happiness which comes from attending to a dead person, when death has struck across the way. They had been robbed of this corpse. As the foreigners entered the garden, the local people went back into their houses.

The others came forward. I went to meet them. A neckerchief had been thrown over my father's face: it was the chest which ought to have been covered. They gathered round me. I cannot understand either Italian or Spanish. They realized this, and after the first excited words they tried to explain things to me in another way. I have never made the attempt, but I imagine that out of many, if not all, animal noises, that of the horse is the most difficult to reproduce. They brayed, they bellowed. I put up my hand to interrupt them. I knew that my father had gone off with the buggy. Then one of them, close-shaven but ill-shaven, with a dirty cap pulled down over his eyes, and a torn leather vest—I had the impression that he was the boldest and most sensitive of them all—joined his hands together and then separated them slightly, bending his fingers except for two which, pointing into the air, moved about. Suddenly he threw his head back, at the same time wagging it from side to side and shutting his eyes. I gathered that the mare too was dead. He was the boldest or the most sensitive of them all. I pointed one finger at my father, then at the door of the house. The man bowed. The others followed him.

My father spent all night and the following day in his office, where I took the foreigners. They stood there for a moment, embarrassed, their arms hanging down at their sides, and went out again without looking at me. They suddenly seemed tired. The steward arrived. I had spent part of my childhood in his company. He had stopped coming to the house. At the age of twenty I had become the master. I told him to see about the remains of the buggy, out on the road to Avignon. The accident had occurred five miles from the village, and it is as far again from there to the town. My father's death being so recent and the memory of his interdictions still fresh, I doubt if he borrowed that car or that pickup truck which we had never had. He must have harnessed the other two mares to the landau, disregarding the plow horses, for I saw him again barely two hours after the foreigners' departure and a good while before that summer night which was the first for me. The steward stayed with me for I wanted him to receive the visitors and show them in: the parish priest, who stayed a long time talking without saying anything, then the pastor, who came out of courtesy or convention, and finally two little groups which followed one after the other, the members of the parish council who are also those of the town council. They looked at their chief churchwarden and their mayor, and I think that they welcomed the evidence of their eyes. In their attitude there was something like relief, a levity which lent a tremulous quality to their gestures, their careful, whispered words. It was late at night. We had the

8

doctor, and after him a few landowners, and later on a few humble folk. I said then to the steward that I was counting on him early the next morning, for from Avignon and the surrounding villages would come all the people who had been informed by their newspaper or by word of mouth of what had happened, and first of all the solicitors of the department, who had elected my father president of their disciplinary chamber. They would be wearing masks of sorrow, those crafty rogues: I guessed that their satisfaction at seeing my father—who had a poor opinion of them and made no secret of the fact—for the last time would be better concealed than the councillors' febrile joy. Not that the peasants, nowadays, are different from the people marked by the town, or that a tricksters' complicity is not being established between them, in an amalgam so rapid that it may now be complete. My father, for his part, knew that this was happening, that under his eyes which wanted and did not want to see, it was in the process of coming about. He had always known. I was left on my own.

I spent the night with the body, rummaging through the papers. I found no trace of the correspondence, copious though it was, which he carried on all over the world with men whom he had come across by chance, whom he had never seen, in most cases, for my father did not travel and people had to come to him, obscure individuals or persons of local fame of whom the press had reported on some occasion, in lower case, a gesture, an action, an observation, and my father had recognized himself, or else they had published a book at the author's expense, memoirs, recollections, nostalgic reveries, meditative, dreamy pages, and my father's booksellers had caught them in their nets, out there in Richmond, Charleston, Niort, Capetown, Brisbane. And I remember that I said "come across by chance" just now, but no it was not by chance, for in the end my father felt such a strong, almost physical need for these people, letters failing to satisfy him any more, that it seems to me that he called them and controlled their movements, and I believe that those rare encounters in the hotels of Avignon, which they promptly left to drive out into the country in the buggy, partook more of an inner compulsion than of a miracle. He wrote a great deal to Virginians, Brazilians, Australians, Georgians although he could not read Russian, a Fuegian from the frontier of Chile, men who were all landed proprietors, and I remember the coincidence, which amused Virginie and amazed me, of a New Zealand planter who was also a solicitor, but for some reason I do not know, I shall try to understand it another time, another night, the thing annoyed my father.

He imagined the other's estate on the outskirts of the village, like ours, its beginning and its end, so that on one side there were the houses and on the other, if not exactly the desert, the jungle, the steppes, at least their approaches and their borders—the remains of a fire, trampled soil, broken branches which a life determined to defend itself against men was already scattering, leveling, rotting—and my father would tell of the old music, the old noises to which he would go and listen every day on his own estate—the whistling of the scythes, the sound of the plowshares striking an obstacle, the exclamations which are not drowned by any machine, the gruff friendship of man for horse—and would tell of the outlying villages skirted by roads whose ruts the local people know by heart, and the trees, the flowers, a sky the sanctuary only of the birds, of real flesh and feather, and I remember my father's delight when his correspondents sent him the drawings he asked for, his anger if he received photographs and I can see him bent over those sketches in which he placed in imagination rivers and mountains, describing them far better, it seemed to me, than the pencil. No, I found nothing, I lost my way among official papers, but I remember the envelopes loaded, over-whelmed with stamps which Virginie and I had never dared to detach. I inspected the books, look-ing through them all. Nothing. I put them back in their places, taking care not to displace the book-marks. Father would mark the pages which formed his reading and, every day before meals, ours. At present these books are the only ones which inter-est me and I too have gotten into the habit of reading aloud, during the day, in the daylight. The night comes more quickly—with the whole of the garden. Just like my father, in fact, and Virginie is right, would be right, except for the fact that nobody listens to me. She has never come back. I know nothing about her, where she is, what she is doing. I have not been able to inform her of the accident. It is as if Virginie were dead. Yes, that is it, Virginie is dead when I am alive.

She was four years my senior and as far back as I can remember she made a great fuss about me, worrying over my silences, over that sort of un-thinking allegiance to my father's ways in which, as she told me again and again, she saw signs of a certain torpor, or resignation, or absentminded-ness, as if I were under discipline, in the position of a disciple, if not of a slave. I liked her as a little girl, without giving much thought to her, although now and then I was surprised to find myself wishing that I had her hair, which was fine and interminable, and her eyes. But I paid attention to no one but my father, or rather not attention, it is attentiveness I want to talk about. Virginie and I each had our own room, which was our playroom and our library, always full of books which our father always chose for us and went on giving us even when Virginie, to his certain knowledge, read others, which she bought herself with the money which our mother gave her for clothes. He would awaken us with a sharp rap on each door, mine first, at six o'clock every morning and we were so used to that hour, to that expectation, that I cannot remember my father ever knocking twice. I never saw my sister washing, for we each of us had our washstand in our room. We breakfasted on coffee, milk, jam, butter, pieces of fried pork which we ate with a fork straight from the dish and rye bread which a neighbor baked for us, in a charcoal oven, as they used to not long ago, I cannot say for sure, in an age which my father had not left and which for us, his wife and the maidservant, Virginie and me, he prolonged by means of those readings I have mentioned, before meals. He had prepared them the day before, or that morning, or else followed a plan laid down over a period of several months, or perhaps several years, thought that it enhanced our pleasure and interest to know the authors awaiting us: accordingly he would skip weeks and months and I can hear him saying: "In April, we shall read *The American Journey*" and "I'm keeping *A Journey in the Black Country* for the holidays" or "*American Notes* are easier to understand in winter, the shit" and I must say here, before going any further, that my father who hated coarse language so much that neither Virginie nor I ever uttered a swearword in his presence, my father, every time he mentioned Dickens, could not help calling him a shit, adding that the Englishman had not understood anything about anything, a numbskull whose influence had been considerable and was still active in that we were blind as a result of his having shut his eyes and his fellows with him, after him, pretentious little travelers, quibbling over details and incapable of appreciating general effects, arrogantly assuming the privilege of being shocked everywhere and all the time away from home, coarse brutes who had failed to grasp the necessity of stopping time about 1842, and if they had made the attempt and succeeded, we should be enjoying eternity, paradise on earth, I mean what my father meant by paradise, millions of Virginias, that small amount, that adequate amount of civilization which we need, great estates planted here and there in the depths of the forests where, busy living without thinking about surviving, the big animals roam. Toward the end, the second half of our story, when I was alone with him, with Virginie gone whom I should not be joining until later, our mother dead and the maidservant after her, he would announce "the shit" and open Dickens.

From his lips there fell words which are like snow today. The simplest words but only he used them, words from the past which our teachers uttered by accident and the streets, the houses, people's hearts were deprived of their pictures, so that with no one to embody them they raised no echoes and, simple though they were, I felt that they were rare and heavy, exciting draperies which linked me to my father. Words which evoked bygone spectacles, forgotten traditions, buried rites, a ruined faith and these words fell from his lips into my visionary ears, fell warm and palpitating, opening on to evening gatherings, community prayers and meditations, choirs, ceremonious sarabands, the open-air banquets which used to follow visits from one farm to another, from one plantation to another, something like a carefree solemnity and it sometimes happened that, turning toward Virginie, toward me, my father would hold back his words swollen with pictures or would repeat them insistently, so that a flock of restless doves would flutter around my head and as he, the bird-catcher, pulled the thread attached to their feet, I would see, at eye level, between heaven and earth, in a lingering vision, girls such as the one my father wanted for me, demure in a crinoline, with an eager heart and the sort of modesty which is no longer to be found, those true maidens who, from their mothers and from fear, had learned the art of waiting.

I have not kept all those words in my head. Virginie has aged me. With her I poked fun at them, chased them away, forgot them, I remember that for two years I played the man and laughed at words, so that I have lost some of the plumpest and most beautiful of those paradise-makers. I can sometimes feel them prowling around me, tempted, perhaps, to rejoin me. They come into the garden at night together with the bats. I can count their letters, but in the end those words always form a lump in my throat. What am I to do? But I remember my father's sentences when he started speaking, at first like a steady surge on which I rocked to and fro, then the sentence expanded, each new word filling it out and pushing it farther on, higher up and when it had reached that altitude at which I expected my father to gasp for breath, it arched its back in a fury and collapsed, huge, dislocated, digging a hole in its fall and I hurriedly tried to bury, so as to find them later on, some of the words which had splashed me, but then the sentence started again, rose again, soon becoming a whirlwind, a cyclone and in fact my father did not run short of breath, his sentences were like those fishermen's nets I have read about which stretch for miles, hanging vertically, held by posts as my father's sentences were by commas, invisible posts, inaudible commas, present supports, hidden supports and that, I believe is the secret of a narrator's art, a novelist's art and not long ago, urged on by my sister, I myself tried to tell this story: Virginia before it changed, about 1842, and we know very little about that perfection, an equilibrium between flora, fauna and ourselves, then we had adequate weapons and men's dreams were flagging but the emigrants took to the sea, crazy hordes of covetous men who wanted nothing but to clear, plant, build, invent, and push back the natural frontiers and the tents became villages, the villages towns, the towns cities and I can see my father, every morning and again before the other two meals, reading the shit from the original text he translated word for word, from six to ten pages of the *American Notes* on which he often commented sentence by sentence so that the reading was always cut up, chopped into pieces by commentaries longer than the passage itself and after Dickens one day, it was Tocqueville the next, Le Père du Poisson or Saint-Jean de Crève-coeur, not to mention that Frances Trollope whom my father hated as much as Dickens for her *Domestic Manners of the Americans* and whom, over the years, he had as it were married to the Englishman, calling her a shit too, I suppose because he could never think of a feminine form for that word. Then we were at liberty to begin lunch. While the monologue lasted, my mother had remained with us, immobile like us but standing at a distance, in the darkest corner of the room, with the maidservant. Once the monologue was interrupted, we were a long time coming back to earth.

Then we would set off for school. He had resigned himself to sending us to school after trying private tutors, for when Virginie was fourteen we had two, one for her, one for me, for three weeks. He had combed the surrounding villages, after ours, and gone even farther afield in search of teachers with certificates, diplomas, degrees, avoiding looking for them in Avignon, but in the end he had to resort to the town and we had masters from church school, undenominational school, and finally *lycée*. My father interviewed these at greater length than the others, in his office, on their first visit. Most of them took matters no further, and from our bedrooms with the doors open we would hear the haughty farewell my father tossed them on the landing. These masters all came in cars or on motorcycles, which they brought to a stop outside the door. Those who came again, the inquisitive, the fanatical, the docile, or the mercenary, seemed to have come all the way from Avignon on foot. They used to park their vehicles some six hundred yards from the house, at the edge of the road and the fields. From our bedroom windows we could see, Virginie and I, that the tutor was on the way. We had time to get ready for him.

My father paid them royally, but the most tenacious of them all, at the rate of three days and six hours a week, gave up after three months. He had become attached to us and I think we returned his affection but this tutor, whose name I have forgotten, found it hard to reconcile what he thought education should be and what my father insisted it must be. Arithmetic and spelling were all right, it was over history and geography that they fell out. My father maintained that France had ceased exist after Napoleon III, England after Victoria, America in 1864. Faced with the other man's inadequacy, he made us write essays on traveling, the berline in France, the stagecoach in Dickens' country, the sleigh in Russia, the American wagons and barges. We had to draw up detailed technical reports on the clarence, the landau, the landaulet, the *pauline*, the buggy, the brougham, the *turgotine*, the phaeton, the surrey, the victoria, the sedan. Out of respect for the tutor, he left it to him to correct them. My father wanted us to be told about bears, wolves, mushrooms and resins. Not— for all that he considered that they should be given a place in our daily routine, as a sort of recreation —fantastic stories, of the kind which, with fairies and so on, risk becoming ridiculous, but precise accounts, based on observation or the reading of observers and my father would place at our tutors' disposal, in the hope that they would make copious notes on them, his copies of Buffon, Fabre, Quatrefages de Bréau and Boucher de Perthes. It was always in vain and several times we took the road to school, the road back to school. But I want to say something about the only girl we had, among all those men. A delightful creature full of gratitude for the interest my father took in her, as solicitous about her as if she had been an orphan, she became enthusiastic about a thesis subject my father imposed on her. It concerned the problems of big estates in Louisiana in the last third of the nineteenth century. Every time she came to the house, after every lesson, he would keep her behind to talk to her, advise her, correct her plan, and add to its amplifications, for in order to help her he read the same books as she, as well as all the books which she did not know, would never know. Marguerite Brunet married when she was a third of the way toward her diploma. She was a country girl and that fact must have counted for a great deal in the vexation my father felt. She married an engineer. My father did not answer the letter in which she informed him that, far from the world of books, she was beginning to live a real life.

Then we would come home from the school at the other end of the village. With more homework to do than I had, and that more difficult than mine, Virginie would leave me. Where school was concerned, she showed learning, a sort of anxiety, a fever, finding in it, perhaps, a kind of personality, possibly solitude, or else, on the contrary, company, I cannot say for sure, but I know that she would come out of her room, in the evening, more self-assured than in the morning, more stubborn and rebellious, whereas I for my part displayed a docility and weakness not far removed from dreaminess and self-effacement. My father, with the spider's web he wove with his words, never really caught anyone but me.

Her world was that of equations, of chemical retorts, of formulas, of grammatical points, of orthographical subtleties. She excelled in analysis and parsing, and when I try to discover what used to go on in her head, I always end up with a ghastly vision of texts in which the sentences are decomposed and the words tortured, stripped, scrubbed. In the end, this skill of hers proved her undoing, just as it nearly proved my undoing and nearly separated me from my father forever. But at that time nobody thought that I should one day fall a prey to that madness.

I would run to the farm with my satchel strapped on my back. To get rid of it I would have had to go through the house, but I had neither the time nor the inclination to make this detour, short though it was, I would toss the satchel into the horses' manger, a good place, almost on a level with my eyes so that when, at dusk, the time came for me to leave the animals, I did not have to look for it and did not risk forgetting it. It lay heavily on the hay and the horses made it sticky with their saliva. This is a bitter smell after a while. People sometimes smelled me without seeing me.

My father spent all his afternoons in a silent exchange with things and animals, and in his footsteps my shadow did not draw a single word from him. It was not that he considered my shadow futile. Those afternoons when I walked behind him across the fields and vineyards of his estate prolonged the readings of the morning and midday and anticipated those of the evening. It was like the reality of a dream after and before the dream of reality. Words were for later, for the enclosed space of the house, where the walls, however big the rooms may be, hinder the migrations of the gaze and make one hollow-eyed, near-sighted. He must have felt that in certain places and at certain times we were more fragile than usual, for he prolonged our evenings as long as we were capable of answering his questions and it seems to me that he was impelled by the ambition, which I shall adopt after him if I have any children, to cleanse us of school, of the age, of time. We each in turn gave him a report on our day and repeated to him, in detail, what our masters and mistresses had tried to teach us and what Virginie in particular had remembered, without any effort, and that was a faculty which so alarmed my father that he neglected me for a while, giving me only cursory attention, until he realized that Virginie was lost and that it was essential to save me, his immortality.

Sometimes my sister and I climbed the stairs with our eyes closed and went to bed already asleep.

I think that he was also afraid of our sleep, about which he never knew anything for we were unaccustomed to talking about that sort of thing and Virginie, without growing tired of the same questions, used to say that she never dreamed and I, for my part, had forgotten my dreams.

At bottom, my father's discourses were not, as I believed in my youthful innocence, simply traps to hold the magic of a past and present time, no, they were also agricultural and household words, dishcloth words and pickax words, which he employed to root out and remove the seeds, I might say the eggs which the world laid in us and if our teachers were the greatest danger, the enemy my father fought openly and explicitly, we also had cause to fear our schoolmates, the street, chance, the air which, over the years, had become so foul and poisonous that my father resorted increasingly to warnings and, along the edge of the garden, in the garden itself, flowerbeds, shrubs, a battle which he ought to have won first in the village council against the councillors who dreamed of nothing but causing trouble, of shifting earth and destroying nests to install water everywhere, to build blocks of apartment houses as in the towns and it was without my father's knowledge that they ordered that notice saying TOWN CENTER and planted it at an intersection of alleyways, a pretentious, blasphemous cross considering that we had three hundred houses at the time and a thousand inhabitants and in view of that I can understand my father giving up hope of saving us both, Virginie so reserved and stubborn and me with nothing but my meekness, which was inexplicable and therefore unreliable, how, how was he to get us to grow up together in Virginia about 1842?

There are hardheaded people who will maintain that it was merely a coincidence, but the fact remains that my father went off with my sister the day she discovered she was a woman. I have the story from her who has often told it to me and we laughed a great deal at the time. But Virginie, taken by surprise and feeling unwell, had said nothing about it. At my father's suggestion, they spent the morning touring the estate, an expedition in which my sister had taken part on several occasions but of which she had not retained a single memory. On the stroke of midday my father had Indiana harnessed to the buggy. After the reading and the meal he got together clothes and provisions, making a careful choice of each, and about two o'clock when I had to set off for school, alone, he was still filling a rucksack and a couple of game-bags. My mother whom I questioned on my return gave me a vague reply; my father spoke to her very little and I cannot remember any conversations between them, except on Monday morning, a few words about the household matters of the week. I think that he considered her old and poisoned by life. They set off in the direction of Cavaillon, from which point, leaving the Durance on their right, they took to the roads leading up into the Lubéron mountains. It was early autumn. They reached Manosque, then, traveling north, the Lure mountains, Mont Ventoux and Malaucène, which the buggy entered on the fifteenth day of the journey, the fifteenth and last for my father and Virginie covered the distance between Malaucène and our house in one stretch, a return journey at breakneck speed according to my sister and she could not tell me, but I think I can understand what had gotten into my father then, a feeling of weariness or re-sentment perhaps for he used the whip and Vir-ginie described to me, in her own words and her own manner, the former commonplace and the lat-ter so prosaic that in order to discover the reality of those two weeks I had to imagine, embroider, work myself up into a fever, a journey which my father intended as a sort of initiation and starting from

Virginie's dry account I pictured that drive through
the mountains of the Lubéron, Lure and Ventoux,
steep roads and the people in their black clothes
may perhaps have understood the reason behind
that horse and carriage which the cars found it
hard to overtake and Indiana never saw them,
simply heard them, a noise which she must have
taken for an angry gust of wind, and my father
left even the country roads but that, undoubtedly,
must have been on purpose and Virginie told me
that he was garrulous then and unpredictable,
dancing with childlike gaiety around the truffle
oaks for he would stop the buggy on the slightest
pretext and they discovered, or my father rediscovered, old coaching houses which had all the
trouble in the world looking like garages so that
they left Indiana and the buggy there, and my
father, with a stride which seemed livelier every
day, and Virginie, aching and exhausted, followed
the sheep tracks with the wind, the sun, forests of
beeches, green oaks and pines, almond trees, olives
and lavender in which my father rolled about, into
which Virginie dropped and they met, at rare intervals for the season was drawing to its close,
flocks of sheep with eloquent shepherds and my
father went into ecstasies at seeing or seeing again
the red-roofed villages under the sumacs and he

27

confided in his daughter that it was like Virginia about 1842, the small amount of civilization we need, so that my sister was afraid that my father would never want to return to the plain but then —it was the evening of the fourteenth day and ever since the morning an eagle had been circling above them, high up in the wind—they found themselves face to face with a team of roadmakers, several dozen men with machines and my father asked questions, curious, thoughtful, shaking his head, suddenly far away from them, from Mont Ventoux, then he looked at Virginie and my sister remembered that gaze of his clearly, years later, it had pierced her shell of fatigue but presumably she did not know how to respond to it, a gaze which probed her, searched her, then my father went away, Virginie at his heels, without saying good-bye, without a word of thanks and I imagine that those men looked for a long time at that bowed figure I picture to myself, in any case according to my sister, according to me, from that moment, the moment of turning back, my father was as in- scrutable and silent as he had been open and talkative on the outward journey and they col- lected Indiana and the buggy and all through the night of that fourteenth day then all through the day of the fifteenth, until six o'clock when they passed through the carriage gateway of the estate, they drove without stopping, this time taking the main road, the one which goes down, often steeply, as far as Carpentras and I can imagine the two lamps at the back of the buggy, two stars jolting about in the night and dying with the day at Carpentras, after that the road is flat as far as Avignon, as far as our village and my father never spoke of those two weeks nor did he ever speak again of Upper Provence, of those mountains of the Lubéron, Lure and Ventoux which after that journey existed only in his memory, in his mind, like the Blue Ridge Mountains, in Virginia about 1842. It was the autumn. A few more days and Virginie went off to the town, as a boarder at the *lycée*.

She used to come back to us on Saturday evenings, leaving again on Sunday before dark or on Monday morning and I had to reckon with her, with her presence which took up a great deal of attention and I remember that when my friends or the neighbors asked me how Virginie was getting along, I replied that she would be there before long, in twenty-four hours, in a couple of days and I felt that things had a beginning, an end. Especially as Virginie's routine was full of oddities, inconsistencies, breaks and upheavals: several times I bumped into her in the house, some masters were away or else it was the day of the medical inspection and she had been taken early, or else again examinations were being held in the *lycée* which had to be supervised by the staff. I never knew whether Virginie was at school or at home, I was not sure of anything any more. She had no timetable and upset our habits. My father had calculated that Virginie would arrive every Saturday at five o'clock. But often I saw her, out of breath, nearly half an hour early: Virginie had hurried all the way. She became capricious and accompanied me to school several times, as she used to in the past, as she used to only recently, for the fun of it I suppose and the pleasure of showing herself, a stranger henceforth, to her old schoolmates. I was perplexed. I found my footing in the morning and it was already evening, then morning again, a day later, a week later and in that alternation of day and night there was something frenzied, I could make out time and its wires which Virginie was pulling, for no particular reason, for the love of life and laughter, the pleasure of accelerating, breaking and entangling. That was the period when I started frantically brushing my teeth. My father himself, either because he had not noticed anything, or because he had not found the right counterstroke right away, made a mistake: one afternoon when I was with him, a message came that Virginie was waiting on the road, with one of the tires of her bicycle punctured. He sent the steward with the buggy and told me to go too. I was angry with him for dismissing me but, discovering my rancor, I decided to die. The steward was pensive and silent. When he saw my tears, he said, "Now then, lad, now then, lad," and shook the reins. Virginie was sitting in a ditch at a bend in the road, hiding so as to surprise us, and we were on top of her before we had seen her. Probably her solitude was beginning to irritate her for she jumped to her feet, gay and excited, her skirt rode up to her waist and both of us, the steward and I, saw Virginie's thighs and her white bloomers, an event which I never mentioned to my sister when later on we spent hours searching the past and I should dearly love to know the reason for that silence, that modesty, but the steward turned around, picked up the bicycle and I stared at the place where Virginie had been sitting, calm and motionless at first, then, as time went by, nervous, restless and the grass was flattened, crushed where her body had been and, while the steward was making the bicycle fast and Virginie was talking to him, laughing and chattering, I saw the plants gradually coming back to life, lifting themselves

31

up again, especially a gramineous plant which its blood was pushing in jerks, in angry jolts which were raising it up, I thought blood then, I think sap now and the plant was tottering as if it had drunk or tasted something which had tired it on the shores of sleep and death and it kept losing a little of the height it had just gained but I could feel that an inexorable force was straightening it up, a force which came from the earth and aimed for the sky, the vertical position which it reached in the end, in a final spasm from which it went on vibrating, a spike which ceased to preoccupy me as soon as the steward, holding the reins, called my name, and we set off again, Virginie sitting erect with her hands on her skirt just over her knees, as women do in our part of the world.

My father ordained that Virginie should not leave the *lycée* except on Saturday, to come home. That is how we came to see her appearing and disappearing from then on with such regularity that it was as if she were always with us and never there. On windy, stormy evenings a lull occurs so abruptly that it makes the mind uneasy, and I remember that we used to prick up our ears at the same time, my father and I, and we would hear a sound of sea and ants, it seemed to us that a relic was being eaten away. But our life was so full that it absorbed Virginie and her rhythm, her salt and her mandibles, a little envelope inside a large one. Time's beat was arrested: I had not left eternity.

All the same I would have liked his readings to be even longer and more frequent. I had endured them until now. Henceforth I asked for them. I dreamed of a reading which would have gone on into sleep. Of a sleep which would have kept us at table, my father and me, wide awake. I was full of pictures and my heart used to beat wildly. But the office, the estate, the village council and the parish council took a great deal of time. My enthusiasm touched him. He arranged a library for me inside his own, clearing some shelves on which he placed, in the order in which I was to read them, his chronicles and travel books. I had all the atlases and a little table in his office. He used to make a silent pretense of looking for me everywhere and, coming into our room where he knew perfectly well I was sitting all the time, he would feign delighted surprise. The lenses of his spectacles misted over. Happiness filled his eyes.

I drew up lists of words which I presented to him in the evening. I used colored pencils to copy them out. In red: Bâton Rouge, Coeur d'Alène. In green: Grande Prairie, Fond du Lac, Prairie du Chien, Mont Laurier. I took care to put a fiery color over the letters of this last name. In sepia: Des Plaines, Des Moines, Boise. I had found a white marking pencil to copy out: Eau Claire, Sault Sainte-Marie and Havre de Grâce. A black one for: Rivière des Loups. We spent a long time looking at these names. Landscapes rose up inside us, huge birds. My father spoke to me about the Burnt-Woods. With the landowners of Virginia, these were the men who caused him the keenest regret.

Men in general I think he loved and hated at the same time. I heard him praise them and curse them. He would have willingly exterminated them at one fell swoop, to create them all over again. My father used to say to me: "They are so slow." It had taken them about a million years to reach Virginia in 1842. But they ought to have appreciated the significance and the value of that slowness, and, as it were, prolonged it. My father, if he had created mankind all over again, would have preserved that slowness in them, those millennial gropings, a long night. He would have changed the race in 1842, the year when it lost what it had waited so long to obtain and obtained in full that year, a sweet, luminous peace so that between the first of January and the thirty-first of December of a single year the dreams of mankind during a million years were consummated and consumed. How could they recover from that catastrophe? My father used to say to me: "I imagine a subtle process of movements backward and forward and if that process had been inaugurated then, time would have gone around in a circle ever since." My father used to say to me: "I have read countless books about birds and trees, and several hundred dealing with a single tree, a single bird. I know no more, as a result, about trees and birds. Nobody knows any more. Men should have come to terms with that mystery. Instead they have uprooted it, destroyed it." And my father used to add: "After that it was the turn of the bison and Indians. Nowadays there is no longer any earth or sky or sea, but only, in estates like ours scattered all over the world, men such as you and I who are trying to rediscover them."

The Burnt-Woods no longer exist, have been exterminated. My father and I used to read over and over again that letter which he had bought at an auction sale in Paris, where he had had to go as a young man to sit for an examination, eight pages written by an English employee of the Hudson Bay Company who referred contemptuously to those half-breeds of the Canadian frontier as: French half-breeds naturalized as Indians. My father used to say to me: "In other words, Indianized Frenchmen, Frenchified Indians, men who were at the center and the forefront of things, ideally placed at

the heart of every conflict, always between passion
and discretion, or between two follies which can-
cel each other out, or, again, between two experi-
ences and two attainments mingling their still
waters so that they should have found there that
equilibrium which I often talk to you about and
think about later, men initiated in the mystery of
animality, animals humanized, all creatures living
a continual exchange which would have deprived
them of their exclusiveness without robbing them
of their nature, the original basis which made them
this rather than that and the bison, during a prairie
fire, would have come and eaten out of your hand,
before returning to their instincts but in the Burnt-
Woods the plague never stopped at the dividing
line between the bloods, the tender spot, the zero
point where they could have reconciled the re-
quirements of a sedentary life with their innate
wanderlust, so that with one of the scales of the
balance outweighing the other by a few drops,
they went on hunting the bison when the settlers
were thinking in terms of fences, hedges, estates
and because of a few drops of blood the Burnt-
Woods of Manitoba and Saskatchewan lost Virginia." And my father used to say, after a pause, as
if the idea pained him: "I hate the Indians. I hate
the Virginians." He used to say too: "Listen, in the

whole history of mankind there are no men who have come closer to eternity than the Burnt-Woods. We shall die as the Burnt-Woods died, because of a few drops too many on one side, a few drops which prevent time from undoing its tapestry."

I for my part saw the bison, like our mares, eating out of my hand and galloping blindly back to their prairies. I could feel that my father was right: men ought to have been created all over again.

I had a few friends. I lost them. My spare time out of school was nearly all spent on the estate, where, when I entered the carriage gateway, my visible subjects were waiting for me on either side, in the sheepfolds and the stables. I governed them by means of gentleness and confidences. These were well received and my decrees did not cause offense. In return I shut my eyes to certain caprices and impulsive actions which I felt were natural to sheep and horses.

At the point where the estate ends, with the fields and the river, there began my provinces of Huronia and Iroquoisia. Here lived my invisible people, and also a few missionaries whom I instinctively distrusted. According to my father they were unavoidable. I had accordingly allowed them into my provinces, but only hand-picked missionaries

37

who, even then, gave me scant satisfaction and the more I learned about them, the more exacting I was. I expelled a great many of them. I searched the luggage of the newcomers to confiscate their firewater. In that way I broke a good many bottles. Finally I sermonized them, urging them to do their work intelligently and patiently. No, the Indians cannot be dressed all at once, at a moment's notice, for fear of contagious diseases. I introduced vaccination into America, I started progress again.

Little by little, day by day, the years went by, eventually a century, then two and three so that about 1810 I had to think about the Burnt-Woods. I conceived them, without compromising the missionaries. I had exactly the number of white men that I felt were needed. I took a wife like the laymen, out of weakness and to avoid being conspicuous. Occasionally I forgot this squaw, the least thought-out of my creatures. In the last weeks of 1841, as I was beginning my thirteenth year, I ordered that race, that people according to my father and myself to cross the borders of our fields and make their way into Virginia. They entered the country in the first days of 1842 and were made welcome. Entertainments were given in their honor; these lasted a long time and would still be going on but for my sister. A sort of active laziness reigned among the Virginians. They listened to bands playing and one day followed another. People took pleasure in talking. When the Burnt-Woods crossed the State frontiers the Virginians had felt a sentence springing to their lips, a graceful sentence studded with commas, shining words which appeared to have been sharpened on spring waters, a sentence which I should still be hearing but for my sister and it seemed to them, with these inexhaustible words and inexhaustible themselves, that they had been raised to the eternity of a sentence without full stops, of a life outside time, its halts, its signs. We knew nothing of full stops and my father had become my tutor. He taught me languages, other ways of speech.

I used to ask him whether one day Greek, Latin, Hebrew, English, German—and the Cherokee and Osage dialects, which he had learned by himself, with the aid of rare bilingual grammars—would no longer have any secrets for me either. My father would laugh. How he loved that question! Even if he had found an answer which nullified it, I would still have asked it, out of affectionate roguishness, for the sake of his laugh. Sometimes when I forgot the question, a recurrent but insignificant obsession, I noticed him maneuvering: "You've made so much progress. . . . You're a high-stepper, a regular hustler. . . . You're mastering the mysteries of language at full speed. . . . One day perhaps you will overtake me. . . ." Then I remembered the question. I cried: "When? When shall I have finished with all these languages?" And my father laughed.

After a pause I joined in. Then he would stop laughing and say: "Never." He repeated the word: I would never overtake him and never know the secret of languages. But there was no need for me to pull a long face. He himself, however far he had gone, and despite the fact that he learned as fast as I did and was in as much of a hurry to arrive as I was, he himself would never master the secret.

He would explain to me: "Words are outside us. Countless words, infinite combinations of phrases which nothing touches, nothing changes, nothing captures: neither your mouth, nor your accent, nor the meaning which you think they possess, which they may possess or not, which you want to give them, which they may take or not and as the evil of each day is sufficient to that day you exult at having trapped three hundred words but think of those that remain and remember that the corpses in your perforated memory, once they have recovered the frenzied life of their myriad meanings, can always slip out, where you may catch them or not and I like the idea that following my example you have joined in a race with them as if we had eternity with us whereas you live in two different times, the words and you, because remember that they already existed in 1842 and that you were not yet born at the time."

That was true.

Then:

"Vain harvests . . . When you have gathered them into the barns which are inside you, think of nothing; then you find lined up beside you the motionless crows that are words and when your memory and your hand open, they fly away in a flurry of wings and meanings. You are left with a few feathers, and also the bodies of those who are shamming death and in the fever of the hunt you fail to see that you lack the essential, the full and unique significance which words assumed in Virginia about 1842 when they inhabited things, and men, as a result of beating the woods and following the flight of the eagle, steeped themselves at the same time in the vision and the meaning of things, and when they had returned home they had only to name what they had seen to hold and retain their vision, an oral possession which satisfied them in full for it was that of things themselves, and the eternity which is in words embraced the

41

whole world but you know what followed: that invasion, starting in 1842, of frustrated men dreaming of roofs and enclosures, dreaming of killings which were already mechanical and the woodcutter's ax felled the forests and the trees which are the high dwelling of words, so that with the chips and shavings the words disappeared, splintered and scattered and, once the year 1842 was over, continued their historic wanderings and ever since have been roaming the world, powerful, disconsolate gamblers, words searching as we are searching, deceived, deceitful words which have as many meanings as they have suffered blows of the ax and which take their appearance from the land where they live, where they settle so that the more languages you know, the better you will be able to remove their masks and imagine that you may perhaps rally them to things. . . . We are going to learn Italian, Spanish, Seminole. . . ."

Then:

"An insane hope . . . We would need eternity to get to know all the words there are, their eternity. The fact remains that with them you are right to go fast and think that you are going to arrive. Progress in words is the only progress which is not mortal. By dint of frequenting them, you may just possibly steal something from them, the smoke as it were of their eternity. . . ."

He would open a file, and I would lean across the table to see:

"Look at the chaos which has reigned since words departed from things. . . . Look at what the Pope's newspapers say, how short of breath he gets, how incompetent he is, manufacturing Latin names to describe new things, to hold them!"

He would laugh, and I would laugh too. I could feel that he was making an effort not to say that the Pope was a sort of Dickens.

Then:

"Sometimes I hear whirlwinds and tumults inside me, my blood suddenly strikes a dam which hurls it forty, fifty years back, back where childhood and birth are to be found and I tell myself, in the joy of this rediscovery and the happiness of my new blood, that it will not flow again, that I shall never die, and then I feel very close to Virginia and I allow myself to think that I really ought to make the journey, for out there, in some corner where men never go, so well hidden that nothing penetrates it, neither light nor darkness nor the seasons, there must be a copse, a thicket where a word unfamiliar to us is sheltering, a very old word which does not travel, eternal in its lair and if I picked it up, I who know, I should stop time and death. . . ."

"And will you take me with you?"

"My blood bursts the dams. . . . I have always

postponed the journey, rejecting the brief illusion of the seething blood for the reality of the house and you know what it was like, when I inherited it, a middle-class house which I had to transform from top to bottom and I can assure you that it went back through time almost wall after wall and I flanked it with porticoes supported by columns which did not exist in my father's time, and the carved balconies, the garden of magnolias, the wisteria and the peristyle as well, I devised everything and you know too that I created the estate as it is today, almost a plantation with the stretches of maize and the small amount of civilization we need, cultivated fields following right after natural prairies, as I learned that they did in Virginia, and for a long time I thought that the words would come back, one day, turning away forever from the thought of that journey which I long for and fear and I planted the right trees, the right fences, with trunks shaped like earthworms as they were in Virginia and I had the course of the river altered, at my expense, so that it passed through the estate and I made our two Indian canoes out of bark, then again I stopped up some hideous horizons where the eye was lacerated by tiled roofs, I made traps to catch the words, but it's too small. . . . The words don't hear when I whistle to them. It's too small

44

and I wonder, what with blood flowing and time passing, whether I didn't make a mistake, whether I shouldn't set fire right away to the estate, to the house. . . ."

I sat there with a lump in my throat while he dreamed.

Then:

"An error of principle and of method . . . I wonder whether I shouldn't have been satisfied with my dreams and pictures, without saying anything, without doing anything, saying and doing anything else, contenting myself with an inner Virginia instead of trying, by the expedient of things, to rediscover it as it was and all the time I have spent reconstructing Virginia, I should have devoted to ripening and caressing it inside me and it would have taken me forty, fifty years but I tell myself that in the end perhaps the real words would have come to me, radiant, definitive, bringing the things with them and I would not be obliged, in order to give force and magic to my necessarily imperfect discourses, to walk around my own miniature Virginia, so that I can never warn you sufficiently against the things which can be seen, which can be heard, which can be touched, the house, the estate which perhaps I ought to set fire to right away. . . . Nobody ever dreams enough."

45

He had accustomed, if not reconciled, the village councillors to meetings after dusk, in summer and winter alike. On Saturdays it was with the parish council. We would eat on his return. I remember that he would close his books, his shadow merging into the darkness of our room, and I waited, motionless, for his hand to stroke my forehead, a furtive caress which he never forgot and then I knew that he had passed by, that he was going off, the door opened and closed, the gravel complained and I heard the garden gate too opening and closing. I would stand up and find my mother at the door of our room: "What did he mean, your father, when he spoke of setting fire to the house and the estate?" I knew perfectly well what I wanted to tell her about: the fire, leaping flames, a flickering red vision, a clean sweep and we should be happy but I could not find the words my father had used as if, when he went away, he had taken them with him and those which rose to my lips showed me to myself indigent and monstrous, words which lit a fire of whose balefulness I suddenly became aware and I should have liked to die of stammering but my mother had long ago resigned herself to not understanding, she went off, her shoulders drooping, to the kitchen where she talked with the maid-servant, who was as old as herself, about the weather, births, deaths, the passers-by in the streets, life like herself.

At the beginning, Virginie used to accompany us to the movies. We soon discovered, my father and I, that we were happier on our own. She came all the same. Then she stopped.

The movie-house managers at Avignon were in the habit of buying property in the countryside around our village. They used to consult my father as the most honest and dependable solicitor available and willingly told him, for he showed an interest in the subject, what films they would be showing weeks and months ahead. Sometimes we would go to Avignon three times in less than a week. We also went a year and a half without seeing a single film.

He liked nothing but Westerns. I liked nothing but Westerns. And then they had to be in color. And then he, and I like him, appreciated only landscapes. We would tell from the first gallops whether the film was going to be rich in landscapes, and if it threatened to be poor, then my father got up, giving the signal for departure. I have seen films from beginning to end, but more often I have seen fragments of films. The idea of leaving almost as soon as we had sat down made Virginie nervous. On the way to the movie house she would beg my father to promise to stay to the end, whatever the film was like. My father would not promise. Virginie lost patience.

When she became a boarder we were relieved of our remorse, our embarrassment even. He told me that in town she could see all the films she liked.

I fretted once over the problem of how we should have managed, in Virginia in 1842, without any Westerns in color. If Virginia had been the real thing? According to my father, we would have had no need of Westerns in color. But he did not exclude the possibility of a sort of peaceful, innocent progress which, on the fringe of the general immobility, would have taken over a century: a man invented a magic lantern, almost without any effort, in order to see somewhere else, in an unimaginable world, things which are no longer real. My father slowly raised his hand and went through the motions of gripping an object, which I guessed to be a screwdriver, and turning it. His hand revolved. "Imagine," he said to me, "that gesture going on for a hundred and fifteen years." His hand dropped. It seemed to us that the mare had come to a standstill.

His clients the movie-house proprietors were a great help to him. A long time in advance my father would tell the village councillors that he was canceling the meeting on a certain day and that all of them, the following day, would work twice as fast. The councillors appreciated this courtesy and took the opportunity to go to the movies too. Their cars would overtake the buggy. A shiver ran along Indiana's spine, her ears twitched, my father saw nothing, heard nothing, I said: "Martel," "Fabre," "Chavasse." Then, once again, there was that mingled music made by horses and a kind of well-being: excitement at the thought of the movie, torpor on account of the mare.

To reach Avignon by the almost entirely level road took less than an hour. Indiana liked these outings in the cool of the evening or the night. I remember that at first my father used to entrust Indiana and the buggy to a bicycle-park attendant who was to be found on a wide pavement in the main street of Avignon. Grown-ups and children used to crowd around to comment on the rig. Our departure, at the end of the film or earlier, was accompanied by shouts and laughter. I hated in silence. I imagined a school like Virginie's in which I fought the others. My father parted company with the bicycle-park attendant. He hired a shed on the outskirts of Avignon, by the market where the sight of a horse aroused hardly any interest. We made our way to the movie house on foot.

49

Then the Westerns went through a bad period. My father did not give up our outings. But it was no longer to attend movies, which we knew would be brief, that he harnessed Indiana. We set off for the sake of the return journey.

We used to choose the dimly lit streets of Avignon to drive along and the banks of the river drew us too. There, before continuing on our way, we waited until after midnight. Martel, Fabre and Chavasse must be far away already. In the suburbs Indiana's hoofs rang out loud and clear, and I imagined balls of music inside them which the impact of the hoofs on the ground hurled against the walls of the sleeping houses from which they had no time to return, in the form of echoes, for other balls were coming regularly from the hoofs, in a gay, rhythmical music which had something about it of a triumphal accompaniment. Then we came out into the open country. The balls of music lost their strength and we abandoned ourselves to the swaying motion of the carriage, we listened to the tinkling bells around Indiana's neck. There was a considerable risk that I would fall asleep after the bridge, where, as soon as we were on it, I leaned over to see us in the water: mare, buggy, the two of us, swift and elongated, phantoms all. Then, in spite of my father's warm proximity, I felt afraid of some dangerous encounter. But my fear vanished. He must be thinking where we should stop. Whether the wind was blowing, or it was raining, or it was a moonlit night, he always stopped.

True, he knew the country well. He could have chosen long beforehand the place, which was always different, where we should stop. But I think that he used to mark it, on the outward journey, with a mental notch.

Turning into a little byroad, Indiana left the main road behind until the growing number of bumps and potholes warned us that if we insisted on going ahead we risked damaging the buggy. We would leave the mare alone with her patience. My father loved dark nights most of all and this love of his was so imperious that he spurned the moon. He often told me that they were quite enough, the two lamps which we should look for at the end of our stroll, when we had reached the top of the hill and that with the moon one is always condemned to daytime sights, as in broad daylight, so why pick the night? We used to set off across the fields and I imagined several compasses in my father's heart, enumerating them under my breath: the compass of what he wants, the compass of what he knows, the compass of what he tries to change, and finally the biggest of all, the compass of his love for me, with a needle which all the needles of all the other compasses imitate and follow, the Mother Goose compass and why did the needle always have to point north? I asked the question and my father gave me a vague explanation. He seemed harassed. When I put the question to him again, later on, he replied that the other end of the needle always pointed south. That is true. My father never made a mistake. He knew where he was going, I had only to follow him.

I was silently excited, but briefly, that he should have chosen me as his companion and that he should change the days to come, so many years, so many centuries for me on my own, since he assured me that he had to die, from frenzied greyhounds into domestic animals. I imagined that my future would follow me, captive, docile and at the back of my throat I said that for the first time when I was about two hundred thirty-five and the second time about six hundred nine, without involving my dead father in any risk, I would tug at the animal's leash, not like Virginie at the time when she used to come home to us from school, for no particular reason and out of stupidity, a desire to live at a greater speed, no, I hurried time on in order to know a detached pleasure, like someone who knows that he risks nothing and can never lose. I hated games and I yielded to a feudality of suspended time in which I alternately caressed and flogged the days, my serfs. Our walk, during which we kept abreast of one another, was a little erratic and one night I realized that my father was allowing the ground to guide us, with its bumps, its potholes, its molehills and animal or geological excavations, we were following the invisible pattern of the earth, carried by it and I felt our utter abandonment to its nature, its whims, the ground under our feet was uneven, as if it had been in an earthquake and the bumps, the potholes bounced us about like bullets, we kept emerging, falling back again, stumbling at its mercy and I knew, that night, that my father's compasses were in the ground as well.

Once we had reached the top of a hill, for this was always the tangible object of our walk, we would make out, after such a straining and opening of the eyes that it seemed as if our ears too were trying to see, a faint yellow light, far below, as if we had left Indiana in a valley and we were on a mountain peak, the two lamps creating only a single candle glow. We stood there, looking at it, as it burned without shedding any light and sometimes we did not dare to recognize it as soon as we saw it, for because of a gust of wind, of life, it seemed to go out. But it was the light sure enough.

One night when it remained invisible for a long time and the eyestrain was beginning to unnerve me, whether because he guessed at my discomfort or because he was sharing it at that moment, my father broke the silence to say to me that it would require truly exceptional strength to put out the light. And that probably nobody possessed that strength. We found the light, although it was raining.

The top of the hill was bare or else a tree was standing in the middle. We would walk around it and, once the inspection had been completed, my father would lie down. I would stretch out beside him, with a space of dead leaves or green leaves between us, or pine needles and once, I remember, acorns. We listened attentively to the night. I enumerated, silently, in order to discover the extent of my vocabulary: mattings, glissades, hissings, creepings. I found, to my delight, words I did not know I carried within me. All produced sounds and were accompanied by pictures, so that in the end the darkness outside struck me as inert and almost dead. There is no truth, incidentally, in those stories I have read of men who lose their way in some wilderness and remain motionless, holding their breath, absent to such a degree that life begins again around them. In the course of those nights I did not see a single wood owl, a single brown owl, and the hares and rabbits I passed were lying at the roadside. I enumerated: hooting, rustling of wings, pineapple eyes, screeching and within me I had, I have always had, countless living wood owls, brown owls, round yellow gazes.

I could see nothing, hear nothing, feel nothing and my father asked me, breaking a lengthy silence: "What can you see, what can you hear, what can you feel?" I said: "Nothing." Then he told me to go to the edge of the hilltop and make sure that the light was still burning. I went as fast as I could, impatient to have done with this test and I returned, beside him, to my warm place and the wood owls, the brown owls, the hares my words. Once again there was silence around us, a tumult within me, with all my animals, and a long time afterward my father asked me: "What can you see, what can you hear, what can you feel?" I froze my senses and seeing nothing, hearing nothing, feeling nothing, I said as much.

I loved my father for having given me a command of a vocabulary for the two of us, outside dictionaries; I used it only for great occasions, the nights when one feels oneself opening and closing at the same time, when one is conscious of abysses. I told him that I was beginning to see, hear, feel.

He answered that so was he but that all that counted was my experience of what we were going to say and do, since he would die, one day, so that . . . for a long time I waited, a long time. Then I said:

I was ripe for death, and by a dangerous road my weakness led me to the limits of the world and of Cimmeria, the land of shadows and whirlwinds,

a sentence which I found by myself and promptly took out of the book to install it, a musician, a starter of images and purveyor of echoes, in my memory where it has been knocking ever since, pestering me to say it while I have been tireless in saying it, and I remember my father when I recited it to him, his amazement, his happiness, his sadness, dreams visited him and he bared his teeth as if he would have liked to bite it and hold it in his mouth, imprison it, a queen-sentence for which I found a suite and without having consulted each other we realized that it had to be made our opening sentence, a ritual measure, so that only the accompanying dicta changed in the course of those nights on the hills and when I had chanted it, feeling the impetus in him as in me, I went on:

How splendid is the light!—The tomb with its cold night—Outrages Nature's day.—Death, choked with dust,—Darkness, chill and fust,—

*Bones, worms, decay,—Stifles in its clay—All our
strength and lust,*

a stanza which he found for me, but I think that,
more than he, I felt that it was made for us who
hated the sun and all the things which remain
when we pass on, so that, reciting it, I planted the
stanza like a sword, then, standing on the hill, I
sobbed and cried out:

*Nature! Nature! The hawk tears the sparrow, the
fig eats the ass and the tapeworm devours the man,*

a sentence which he had read and underlined, but
it had not arrested him whereas I had promptly become its partisan, vaguely loving in it its associa-
tion of innocence with an eternity which I tended
now to believe that of life, now that of death, perhaps both together, how could I tell, loving it con-
sciously for propelling us with dreams and visions
into a province in the air on a level with our heads
in which we found Virginia about 1842, and with
time and evil overwhelmed, and this sentence
spoken, which was burning our blood, I unfolded a
calm apocalypse, adding to the first stanza:

*Fish, waves and bars,—Ships and their tars,—
Tritons and Neptune,—Will not abide—On their
backs will not ride—The chariot of Fortune,—And
the power of the moon—Will abandon the tide.*

*The planets will halt,—Earth turn to salt—In
this splendid structure—Which Heaven has made.
—What is seen here and said—Will pass in the future.—The weakness of Nature—Will let all things
fade,*

forming a whole which he too had learned by heart
and in the dark I saw without seeing them his lips
moving, then my voice dropped to say:

*Yet it must be admitted that nothing is clarified
by speaking here of magic or ecstasy, the charmed
stone, the familiar animal. Nothing is said clearly
by speaking of the ineffable. Nothing is admitted
by speaking of secrets,*

a sentence which I had not read at the time, for it
was by an author who was too difficult for me and
I learned it from my father, but I decided on my
own that it should be, as often as possible, our
finale, perhaps because I felt it as a sort of lullaby
and it soothed our excitement, drowsy with the refrain: "Nothing . . . Nothing . . . ," which kept us
up to it, up to the level of our heads between
heaven and earth, a place where the darkness, the
hill and the idea we had of ourselves all grew dim:
gorged and bloated with all the words and all the
sentences I had thrown off, we walked along, in

Virginia about 1842, through gardens which were prairies with wild horses which looked at us affectionately and, talking together, my father and I spelled out pictures born of our blended childhood:

Noah, his Ark, his animals, the wolf with the lamb.

Sailing up the Mississippi, the Arkansas, the Canadian River, the Red River, the paddle steamers which transported, deported the Choctaws, the Chickasaws, the Cherokees, the Creeks, the Seminoles to the Oklahoma reserves;

and, drenched in water, the trail of tears;

fourteen thousand Acadians who give the name of "The Great Expulsion" to the genocide practiced on them by the English newly arrived in Nova Scotia and those who escape from the boats, in which their persecutors have installed them so that they should starve to death, travel to Louisiana, where, a century later in 1842, and so far ahead of them that in their weariness from journeying such long distances they choose to shut their eyes, they see a supernatural dawn fall on the frontiers of Virginia.

The Micmacs joining with the whites to exterminate the Beothuks of Newfoundland then, when the Micmacs in their turn have been exterminated, the whites left on their own to exterminate the whales.

My father used to say in a soft voice: "Out there, on the ground, at the foot of the hills, because of the passing of time, mankind lost its memory."

Then: the hordes of Attila, of Genghis Khan, of Napoleon advancing as before, but with metallic noises.

A world without grass.

Piles of old people like piles of refuse and who were going to die and did not know it, and others who knew it and thought it was unavoidable.

Children who were born, became adults, old people, without hope, without help.

False suns, false moons, false stars, everything false, that was obvious here in our Virginia, but out there at the foot of the hills, how could they, the others, tell that all that was false since it went on shining after them?

The great expulsions of the Jews, three in three centuries, from England in 1290, from France in 1394, from Spain in 1492.

And my father asking me: "How many beautiful pictures? How many sad ones?"

And I: "Only one beautiful one, Noah, his Ark, the wolf with the lamb." And my father saying: "Not for long."

We were treading lush, dry grass, the horses a joyful, spirited court around us, when we stopped two magic carpets from Persia ridden by wizards, unceremonious people who hoisted us up behind them for a flight as high as the eagles we touched on our way, their eyes half-closed and bodies stiffening under the caress like cats then, flying side by side at ground level, my father and I, we discussed the land at the foot of the hills, the hideous Cimmeria all over the world, where everything is dark, where people die, full of tombs and graves, where no one digs except to bury, cemeteries haunted by hawks, the terror of the sparrows, and gorged with maggots whose blood is an acid which turns flesh into dung, into manure, so that whatever lives has its roots and strength in putrefaction, the fig in a dead ass, the tapeworm in a dead man and we looked down from our lofty position at mankind indefatigably repeating its tricks: magic, ecstasy, charmed stone, familiar animal, invocations to the ineffable, evocations of secrets, age-old foibles which my father derided to the tune of a song: "Nothing is clarified . . . nothing is said . . . nothing is admitted . . ." then, when the three stanzas had swarmed out of their hive our memory, God appeared before us from a recollection of catechism class, with a bushy beard, splendid white veils, outstretched arms and stopped the course of the world in a dawn already splashed with sunlight.

We had to get up, live, put out the lamps. With our hands cupped around our aching eyes, we tried to hold back the night. Mad fish and other pictures spun around in my head as if speed could preserve them from the light and I remember the last picture, on the hill, a rather allegorical wicker trap which was withdrawing, receding and, raking land and sea, was taking back to Virginia about 1842, where they piled up on one another, ships with their keels in the air, disembowled cars, shattered planes. The bells were ringing for Matins and, between each sound, a vague murmur rose to our ears. We listened to it, to its sweet stammerings, we would have pitied it, we would have loved it, had we not known that it was sly and artful, already big with the hubbub and the tumult which, a bad seed, a mortal seed, blossom out in broad daylight. Despite the insects, Indiana looked as if roots were holding her by the hoofs. She had not moved an inch and I told myself that all night she too had been haunted by visions. The tugging of the reins made her rear up. Exasperated, she rediscovered the bit. My father started turning the buggy. I watched his clumsy movements, he made a mistake, he had to begin again, it was a long business. Finally we drove out onto the road.

We were four, five, six miles from the village. If he had hurried Indiana, I think she would have taken no notice. I relaxed, but it was not the same any more. My voice must have been scarcely audible, for I remember my father saying: "What?" "What?" I was asking: "When shall I see the St. John's wort with the yellow flowers, the hollyhocks with the pink plumes, the purple-crested obelarias, the cone-shaped Oenothera, the liquidambars, the Carolina poplars?" I went on but my desire for knowledge was even less perceptible than before for he kept saying: "What?" "What?" and I: "The boumìers, the Calycanthuses, the blue wood pigeons, a coat made of animal skin?" Extraordinary words, fervor in *The American Journey* and always at times of distress or drowsiness, this sentence runs and plays on my teeth: "They hoisted me with halters up an otter path."

When we came to the first houses in the village, he seemed to remember my questions: "It's nothing and it's as you like it, as you see it. If you saw them as they are, all those things, you would be disappointed. You would lose confidence in words. You would not be able to say them any more. You would be alone."

As soon as we opened the door of the house I could sense my mother, the maidservant standing in the kitchen, on the lookout. I went upstairs to bed. My father, in the stables, unharnessed Indiana and rubbed her down. She too would sleep while he was receiving clients in his office.

In the end I stopped going to the river, I neglected the canoes, besides, my father seemed pleased that I should abandon the estate. I read two, three books a day, I learned by heart the most beautiful pages, sometimes just sentences and words which I recited aloud in my bedroom with the shutters closed, just a space to let in a little light, enough to read by without straining my eyes, the books hid me although I was growing.

There had been a war, the one we had with the Germans. It lasted four years. In the village itself there were people who were short of food, the laborers who, doubtless sick of digging all day, hated their gardens. My father helped them. He remained mayor all the time there was the war and the Germans. I never saw them, they did not come to the village, nor to the surrounding villages. For two whole days we heard gunfire. It was the landing and, all around us, the same life went on, perhaps with a little more vibration in it, as when a shiver runs along Indiana's spine. We did not talk about the things of the world and nothing in my father's conversation revealed, as did an expression I surprised, that he read the newspapers eagerly. One morning, however, when I was in my room, I heard shouting outside. As it grew louder I ran to the window. A dozen people were gesticulating outside the garden gate, but at a distance. I sensed that they were shouting insults. I tried in vain to recognize the men, the women. Yet they were people from the village, the very ones, I realized that right away, whom my father had helped in the difficult days not long ago, only yesterday.

He was not there. How could I tell him to delay his arrival, especially now that the shouting was dying away, tailing off? Just then my father appeared. The group fell silent, wavered. He spoke to them, from my room I imagined his lips, then they all held out their hands, my father had finished his speech. I felt him hesitate, finally he shook hands with them.

I should have liked to stay at home the day he appeared in court. My father insisted on having me near him. We harnessed Indiana early in the morning. The judge asked my father: "Why did you go on performing your duties as mayor during the occupation?" He replied: "Because of the fowling pieces. I was the only man who could insist on them being handed in. And every man who owned a gun gave it to me. I stored them in a room in the *Mairie,* which I locked. The guns are still there. And now it is as if the taste for shooting has been lost. I hope it has been lost for good in my village. The men have not asked me for their guns back." The judge went on: "Why?" And my father answered: "The birds . . ." I remember that the judge put his hand to his forehead and my father misunderstood that gesture. He thought that the judge was ordering him to interrupt what he was saying. Everybody in the courtroom was silent. I think that all of them, the judge, his assessors, the defense counsel, who had been appointed by the court for my father did not want one, were suddenly full of pictures of birds. I knew which ones were crossing my father's mind at that moment: eagles. He used to buy them at a huge price, when they were still eaglets, from the two Alpinists who, once a year, around Easter, knocked on our door, with the eaglets in cages, one eaglet to a cage. Every time there were four or five. My father used to release them on the estate, at dead of night so that the bird should not know where to go and we always had one eagle who got used to the place, or almost used to it for I remember, now and then, that a shadow would blot out the sun and I would say: "The eagle, its wings." The judge acquitted him. He remained mayor.

66

That year the summer was so hot that I can single out that year from the rest, that summer from all the summers I have known. It was drawing to its end and Virginie, who was due to enter the University, was spending September with us. She had no examinations to study for but studied all the same and, absorbed in her work, rarely left her room. Sometimes I passed her on the stairs, in a corridor, because of her reserve and the darkness we cultivated, all shutters closed, she was a silhouette. During the meals and readings she spoke so little and in the big room the darkness concealed us so well from one another that only my father seemed to be alive, a high-pitched, clear, tireless voice. The heat weighed on my eyelids. Forgetting Virginie, I also forgot that millions of children and adults were on vacation. Now that I had lost my passion for roaming the estate, I spent with the books in my father's office, sometimes alone and sometimes in his company, the hours I did not devote to the books in my room.

One day that year and that summer when it was so hot, perhaps the shutters had been closed even tighter than usual—we were starting the meal, my father had translated, with an ease which seemed to add something to them, three wonderful pages from Benjamin Franklin's *Information to Those*

Who Would Remove to America, so that, a prey
to pictures, I was a long way from the table—the
maidservant, who was coming in with a dish,
slipped and fell. We discussed the incident after
opening the shutters a little way. Virginie observed
that she was getting old. She repeated: "She is
getting old," without pressing the point, as if without thinking about it. My father who, jumping up
from his chair as soon as he heard the noise, had
helped the maidservant to her feet and gone back
to his place, did not take up her remark. As for me,
when I returned to my lunch I was short of breath,
my heart was beating. It was then, oblivious of the
heat, that I saw Virginie, more than a silhouette.
She was staring at me and I remember thinking to
myself that her eyes were bright and her gaze
vague. I had the impression that, inside me, she
was inspecting my person. Then she looked away,
smiling. If my father had behaved like that, I
would have asked him why, in the course of one
of our conversations.

However much I distrust my longing for transi-
tions and continuity, in which I find an echo of
that hatred which my father felt for hiatuses, for
breaks, for instance holidays cut time in two, in a
hundred, in even more, you say "another week,
another five days, another one, tomorrow," how,

after that, can you escape from death, however much I distrust that longing, I believe that the old maidservant's fall foreshadowed another fall—the end of an order. Our mother died. She passed away discreetly, as dead in death as she had been in life and careful, so to speak, to cause as little trouble as possible to both our life and time. It happened one night, or perhaps during the evening and perhaps my father knew, if he questioned the doctor, the approximate hour of death. He never mentioned it to me, I never thought of asking him. Probably Virginie too showed no curiosity. Later on, when we spoke of our mother, it was always flippantly, gaily, and with an effort of memory.

It was the maidservant who found her, my mother having broken, for the first time that morning, her habit of coming down at six o'clock to the kitchen, where the two women used to meet. The maidservant went upstairs, if one is to believe her story but I think that she had no sense of time and for her the days and nights added up and did not follow on, about ten past six. She too was afraid of changes of rhythm. She must have experienced at one and the same time the feeling of death and that of time, a revelation, a crack of the whip. We sensed that the maidservant was unhappy and several times we saw her crying, hiding her tears from us.

We knew nothing of the ceremonies of death. The maidservant draped the mirrors in the dead woman's room and grouped candles around the bed. The callers were received in my father's office, where all three of us waited for them, he, Virginie, myself. The people from the upper village appeared first, then those from the lower village. Virginie and I felt that they were embarrassed after a few phrases. They glanced up at the ceiling and the women, bolder spirits, turned around to look swiftly at the stairwell which could be seen through the open door of the office, right behind them. My father did not invite anyone to go upstairs and no one dared express a wish to do so.

The parish priest was the only stranger to make the sign of the cross, with the aspergillum. We copied him. I am not counting the maidservant, who went into the room on the slightest pretext, blessing the body every time.

When I was sure that nobody else was going to come, I decided to go upstairs. My legs were numb. All morning Virginie and I had remained seated beside my father. At first, we listened to the remarks, rare remarks as I have already said, which the callers exchanged with him. Sometimes too they spoke to Virginie. Then I allowed my attention to be absorbed by the spines of the books. I was quite a long way from them and, because of the darkness and incipient shortsightedness, I could not read the titles. I tried to guess them. It is a fascinating game. Virginie asked me what I was thinking about, I told her what I was doing. She wanted to follow my example and I knew that I was far better equipped than she was. As it would have been unseemly to get up every few moments to see who was winning, we took some sheets of paper and some pencils and, each on his own, we set out to reconstruct the whole library, several thousand volumes. We began with the shelves in front of us, working from the top to the bottom and from right to left, afterward would come the bookcases on the right and, later on, the shelves on the left, next to the door. I should have liked ten thousand callers, one by one. With one accord we excluded the books behind us, it would have been a simple matter to cheat, by turning around one can easily read the titles for those books are close to the desk. At one point my father, intrigued, took a look at our sheets of paper. He understood the game straight away, took a fancy to it on the spot. In between a couple of visitors, he would go to the far end of the room and call out: "Ten" or "Thirty" or "One hundred and seven." Now one, now the other would be the first to trumpet the title of the book, the name of the author, which we had written on our sheets of paper, with a number. My father nodded in approval (this was for me) and shook his head in reproof (this was for Virginie). My sister was not very gifted. But she tried hard to guess right. As dusk was falling, we had to open the shutters, we were a long way from having finished.

With the night my excitement abated and I felt a desire to see my mother. I closed the door behind me and stood there, for a long time I think, in that room which I should probably not have recognized even if I had been familiar with it. With the draped mirrors, the lighted candles, a kind of smell, the room seemed odd. I tried to compare it with something, I racked my imagination, I found nothing that resembled it. I thought of maggots, of the swinging game they are so fond of, hanging onto the edge of a hole in the eyelid and letting their soft bodies dangle. In the old days I had pushed my schoolmates on swings until I was out of breath, and when I was out of it, it was my turn to be pushed. I pictured ringed maggots hanging onto the lids of my two eyes and I reflected that nobody ever pushed them, so that the maggots fall when they have nibbled too big a hole in the eyelid, fall onto the body or else, if they are unlucky into the bottom of the coffin and it is a huge task to climb up again, to scale the body, to crawl along it as far as the finishing line formed by the torn eyelids, bloody with white blood. I murmured to myself: "A huge task." The expression hung onto me and the two of us stood there looking at my mother, for a long time I think.

How many stories about funerals I have read! Books are full of them, even those which come from Virginia. I knew that the relatives always cry, walking just behind the hearse. None of us cried, except the maidservant but she had been crying since the day before, in any case she stayed behind.

The funeral took place the morning after the death, and we spent the afternoon of that day, my father and I, in his office. I picked up my books again and he his. We saw Virginie again at supper. My father read.

As we were about to leave the table, Virginie asked a question: whether we were going to keep the maidservant. My father looked surprised. I was. He had obviously never thought that his wife's death would lead to the retirement of the only person we had left to run the house. All the same he did not get up and we saw him thinking. Anxious and curious, I then noticed Virginie, she was looking at me with the same bright eyes, the same vague gaze as on the day the maidservant had fallen, I felt that Virginie was at once attentive to me and far away. I had the impression that once again, affectionate and absentminded or condescending, she was inspecting me, inside and remorselessly. Virginie did not give my father time to answer her first question before she asked the second: "And him?"

She meant me. I was frightened. I opened my mouth to say something about myself. This time my father did not seem at all disturbed. I saw his lips part for a smile or some words, nothing else. Nothing in his face moved and I realized that, for some time past, he had regarded me in an unusual way which I had never suspected.

He gently ordered me to go into his office and to wait there, with the books, until he called me back. He told me that perhaps, henceforth, I would not be reading them much any more. They stayed a long time together, the two of them, for over a hundred pages of the *Travels Through North and South Carolina, Georgia, East and West Florida, the Cherokee Country, the Extensive Territories of the Muscogulges, or Creek Confederacy, and the*

Country of the Chactaws, by William Bartram, translated from the English by P.V. Benoist, *chez* Maradan, Paris, Year IX. Then Virginie came to get me. She came in without knocking and I looked up, tall and beautiful my sister was, with pink cheeks, aglow like somebody who had been exerting himself, has been talking a great deal.

I found my father with his back to me, bent, bowed, him who was so strong a shrunken figure and I remembered Virginie's remark that the maidservant was old, my father was holding his hands flat against his face and we used to protect our eyes like that on the hills when the sun was rising. I searched my memory, when was the last time we had gone out? But those nights were so similar that I was unable to single out the detail which would have broken the sequence of time. Virginie told me later that I had been thinking so hard about something that I had unconsciously copied my father and, like him, put both hands over my face, my open palms pressed over my eyes.

They must have agreed without much difficulty on Montpellier. Since it was at Montpellier that Virginie was going to begin studying medicine. I should not be all alone, I should be with my sister and it went without saying and my father kept repeating that I should come home every Wednesday night, every Saturday night, and for the whole of the holidays. He looked through a calendar, he would never have thought there were so many! Cheering up, my father said that he would make lightning trips, so to speak, during the night and the early morning with Indiana, he pictured himself waking us up unexpectedly on days when time was hanging heavy on his hands. I heard a brief laugh, which hurt me. If I had had then the vocabulary I possess today, I would have thrown my arms round his neck. I would have told him that the time which he meant to hurry up like that, alone, on my account, in order to see me, we would bring back, the two of us accomplices, to its previous slowness. Yes, I lacked that vocabulary.

I was informed of the gist of their discussion: Virginie was to leave the very next day, traveling by bus from our village to Nîmes, then from Nîmes to Montpellier by train. She would go to see the headmaster of the *lycée* and enroll me. She would find us two rooms on the same landing. We would always be together, the two of us and, whenever my father came, the three of us. In the morning, she would set off for the University, I for the *lycée*. We would meet for lunch which she would cook, quickly. We would eat badly. She would make up for that in the evening. And on the days we had our father with us, he would do the cooking. During the holidays we would forget that breathless life. Montpellier was much better for us all than the *lycée* at Avignon where I would have been alone, where I would have had to go by bicycle, over twenty miles there and back, and then, after all, we lived in the Gard, on the other side of the Rhône. With his hands flat on the table, my father gazed in front of him, erect, smiling. I gave Virginie an affectionate nod. Dusk was falling, my father got up to light the lamps.

With two suitcases lying open in my room, I often thought, in the days preceding our departure, about the new life which was waiting for me. I filled them with the books, the objects, the personal effects which I prized or which attracted my attention. Virginie did not help me. She would come in, ask: "How are you getting on, old boy?" Glance into the suitcases, and rummage around in them, with no regard for tidiness. I even think that she liked turning everything upside down. But Virginie made no comment. She left me at liberty. The day before we were due to leave, my suitcases were full and I could have used a third. Virginie said: "Pack everything you want." She offered me her suitcases, which were three-quarters empty. She also spoke to me about our rooms, in a tone of voice which, until then, I had not noticed: sharp, curt, imperious. She said to me once: "Two rooms side by side. Big, light rooms, looking out onto a boulevard where cars are passing all the time. But we are on the fifth floor. All you hear there is a vague murmur. Very pleasant. You'll see, you'll like it."

Up to our departure I went on dividing my time between my room and the office, alone in the one, with my father in the other. He had received, in duplicate, some new bilingual grammars which contained some famous texts. It went without saying that I was to take half of these books with me and continue, on my own, my study of Indian languages and dialects. If I had stayed, we would have begun Queshuan. He told me so, but without pressing the point. He would correct my exercises on Wednesday and Saturday nights. He would assign me some more on the Thursdays and Sundays and we would do a little work too on the mornings when he came unexpectedly. I would write in all the languages I knew. "Every other day," my father told me. I promised. This idea appealed to him: that on the days when he left us to return home, he would find on his arrival a letter from me, perhaps two. We expected wonders from whimsical postmen and were afraid that that was what they would be. At least I was not to tell him, when I came, whether I had written to him the day before.

I think that Virginie did all she could to dissuade him from taking us to Nîmes in the buggy. She wanted to go by bus. But the thing seemed so natural to my father that, in front of me at least, Virginie refrained from arguing. When he announced that the buggy was waiting, that six o'clock had already struck, and that Indiana had hurt a pastern, Virginie shrugged her shoulders. My father did not notice.

Indiana, however, kept up a steady trot all the way. We kissed my father good-bye at Nîmes station. He was in a hurry to return home. I thought we were going to take the train, but Virginie, doubtless out of stubbornness, had chosen the bus. The crowd was already pushing forward and when I turned around, after our hurried kisses, for a last glimpse of my father, the buggy had gone.

Virginie said nothing to me, or scarcely anything, during the whole journey. I gazed inquisitively at the scenery, I had never seen it go so fast. When we had gone about halfway, I felt sick. This annoyed Virginie, I ought not to have told her. As I felt worse and worse, despite my efforts to draw deep breaths, I appealed to her again. "Control yourself, for God's sake!" It was her brusqueness, I imagine, that froze the lump which I could feel going up and down inside me. We were lucky enough to find the gates closed at the three grade crossings between Nîmes and Montpellier. I got out each time, I regained my composure.

Shortly before we arrived, Virginie stood up, gathering together her things, a jacket, a silk scarf, some gloves which she had placed next to her own seat. I followed her. But some other passengers had stood up too, separating me from Virginie, who was the first to get out. When I set foot on the ground, she was already holding her two suitcases. I joined her and waited, thinking that someone would hand me my two. Virginie was cross with me again. She showed me my luggage which was waiting a few yards away. I ran to get it. She told me that I ought to be quicker, wider awake, more alive to things. Those were her words. I followed on my sister's heels.

The two rooms were just as she had described them. We went into Virginie's which I liked right away. My sister promptly threw herself on the bed, the size of which struck me. If not three, at least two people could sleep in it. Virginie, stretched out at full length, shut her eyes, then opened them, then shut them again, then opened them again, a game which was not really a game, and which she repeated a dozen times at least. I was standing beside her, I had seen the two blue armchairs near the window, but the idea of sitting down had not occurred to me. She brought me back to things abruptly: "Yokel." Then: "Shit." Then: "Little shit." I sat down hurriedly. My sister had said the words at top speed but she lingered a little, affectionately I think, on the last term. My hands were numb, on account of the suitcases. I wanted to see my room, which was just next door. Virginie ordered me to wait. We remained silent for quite a while, I shut my eyes, I pictured to myself Indiana, my father, our books, the hills. Virginie woke up: "We're fine." A little later: "We'll be fine." I thought so, I was pleased to hear my sister say so. I got up to kiss her. She laughed and confided in me: "I'm happy to be with you. I hate solitude. We'll work hard; we'll have our meals here together. You'll go to your room to sleep and rest. Mine would really have been enough for us, it's so big. . . ." I was looking at her, she fell asleep.

I waited, once again I pictured to myself Indiana, my father, the books, the hills, then the Westerns, the vast blue sky above the green prairies dotted with yellow trees, for it is always autumn in the South. Virginie woke up, she made some coffee, I would have preferred tea, as at home. Virginie said: "From now on, nothing but coffee." Tears came into my eyes, ridiculous tears, for I quite liked coffee too. My sister threw her arms around me and kissed me, she realized that I hated my tears, she said: "It's nothing, the change."

My room was much smaller than Virginie's. I had imagined rows of shelves and there was nothing on the walls. She left me, I took out the note-paper my father had given me, big heavy sheets and yet fine-grained, he kept this paper for his friends all over the world, the landowners with the big estates. I asked him to bring me some shelves when he came to see us.

The next day was the first day of the school year. That morning I woke up at six o'clock, as at home and I did not dare to move, for fear that Virginie would scold me. I put my ear to the wall, I heard her breathing. Virginie was asleep. At seven o'clock I jumped out of bed and, after washing and dressing, I knocked on her door. One knock and she answered. My sister told me that I was not to knock any more, in the future, that it was useless and ridiculous, we were brother and sister weren't we? And then she would like me to wash and dress, every morning, in her room, which was ours, she loved the sound of the water and she had often thought it was absurd, at home, having those two washstands. Besides, mine, here, would get stopped up, she was sure of that, she could feel it. Looking at Virginie stretched out in her bed and chattering away, I was surprised, without telling her, to see that her eyes were wide open and bright, as if she had been awake a long time. I sat down in one of the armchairs and waited. My sister told me to make breakfast. I realized at that moment that I had been expecting her to make it. While I was bustling about I listened to Virginia, she was not going to get up before ten and would go back to sleep after I had left. She would have her breakfast in bed. Ten minutes went by, perhaps less. Suddenly I felt Virginie beside me, she was swinging her arms like a windmill, she was yawning, her nightdress was long and white. Virginie kissed me, we had our breakfast at the table, sitting opposite each other. Busy as I was, I had not seen her getting dressed.

She kissed me again when I left her, in the doorway. On the trip she had made to Montpellier in agreement with my father, Virginie had seen to all the formalities which precede a new boy's admission to a school. I did not have to go to see anybody. I arrived at the school just before eight o'clock. I had forgotten everything, even the shouting, the noise, the running, the quarrels. But nothing surprised me.

Four masters came and went in four hours. Apparently I was not the only new boy in my class. The pupils asked me my name. Several of them asked me more than once, as if it were difficult to remember.

When I got back I knocked on Virginie's door. Then I remembered that she had told me to go in without knocking. I could not see Virginie, the bed was untidy, I had made mine before going out. On the table was a sheet of paper meant for me: "Darling, I have gone back home. I shall come back in a few days." I remembered right away that Virginie's classes did not begin until November for she was starting at the University. Consequently she had nothing to occupy her here. I looked for and found the key to her room, I locked it, since Virginie had gone, I would stay all the time in mine.

Father appeared the following morning, that is the second day of the term. It was still dark, about five o'clock in the morning. I heard Indiana and ran to the window. I waved excitedly to my father, he answered me with a nod and I think that he was smiling. He had received my letter and the buggy was full of shelves. I ran downstairs to meet him.

The buggy contained a couple of trunks as well. My father told me that they were crammed with books. We carried everything upstairs and once the coming and going was over, I opened them. Most of the volumes he had just received. I read the titles out loud, slowly, and we listened in delight to the silken music made by:

(1) Sanson of Abbeville: America in several new and exact maps, etc. and diverse geographical and historical treatises. In which are described succinctly and with excellent, simple method, its empires, kingdoms, states etc. . . , the manners, languages, religions, commerce and wealth of its peoples, etc. And all that is most beautiful and rare in all its parts and its isles. *Paris, Sold by the author, Ruë S.Jacques à l'Espérance* (1656),

(2) Beltrami (J.C.): The Discovery of the Sources of the Mississippi and Bloody River; with a description of the whole course of the former, and critico-philosophical observations on the manners, religion, superstitions, dress, number, origins, etc., of several Indian tribes. *New Orleans, Benj. Lévy* (1824), a work written in the form of letters addressed to Countess Compagnoni and which my father's bookseller at Tallahassee (Florida) had considered interesting, then

(3) Mark Catesby: The Natural History of Caro-

lina, Florida, and the Bahama Islands: Containing the figures of Birds, Beasts. Fishes, Serpents, Insects and Plants: etc . . . *Revis'd by Mr. Edwards, London, Printed for C. Marsh, T. Wilcox, and B. Stichall, 1724,* a work in two volumes and I reflected that I would leave him the first and keep the second, so as not to waste time, then

(4) Hugh Jones: The Present State of Virginia, Giving a particular Account of the Indian, English, and Negroe Inhabitants of the Colony. From whence is inferred a short view of Maryland and North Carolina, etc. *New York, reprinted for J.Sabin, 1862,* then

(5) Gabriel Théodat Sagard, Recollect of St. Francis: The Great Journey through the Land of the Hurons, situated in America near the freshwater sea, at the farthest limits of New France, or Canada. With a Dictionary of the Huron language, for the use of those who have cause to travel in the country and have no intelligence of the aforesaid language. *Paris, Denys Morev, 1632,* a work which my father had been lucky to receive for the Customs had opened the parcel which came from Toronto (Canada), they could have confiscated it, they simply delayed it, then

Others, others, all with engravings, plates in color: I was beginning, in my head, to arrange them on the shelves but my father warned me that only half of them were for me, thirty-nine and he was going to take back the others which he had just wanted to show me. We talked about those he was lending me. We agreed that, once I had finished a book, I would mail it to him right away. And he would do the same with all the works he received. So that, as well as our letters, there would be packages passing between us. We would not mention, in our correspondence or our conversations, the titles of the books we had finished and we would never know in advance precisely what marvel the wrapping paper covered. We were very happy.

I started getting ready and my father went into Virginie's room. He did not stay long. I had to set off for school. Because of the cars, my father moved the buggy. We passed one another, I on my way to school, he on his way to our rooms. And I saw Indiana again, from a distance, on the terrace in front of the station, a sort of replica of the terrace at Avignon.

He cooked the midday meal which we ate together in my room, face to face. Then we decided to go for a walk. He knew nobody here, he did not need to keep on raising his hat as at Avignon. We heard five o'clock strike. He spoke of setting off, especially as Indiana was getting old. We were sad because of us, time, the mare. I calculated that she had to cover ninety miles here and back. However good a trotter she was, it was a long journey.

I would have liked my father to stay all day and not leave until dawn the next day. He would have been comfortable in Virginie's bed. But I did not dare to ask him.

Father came back twice. Then, one evening, Virginie.

I had rather forgotten her. I mean that I did not think about her, busy as I was with my books and classes. If she had not reappeared, I would have taken a long time to notice, the whole of my life perhaps. Yet her absence—I measured it with the help of a calendar, from that date which I remember well, the First of October—lasted only a week.

I gave a cry when I found her in my room which we left right away, her hand gripping mine she pulled me after her. She had put on makeup, red on her lips, black on her eyebrows, green along the edges of her eyelids, nothing but bold strokes which clashed violently with her delicate, white, oval features so that Virginie was wearing a face and parts of a mask, I told her so and that she had two heads. We were scarcely inside her room before she came out again, still pulling me along, she pushed open my door, still holding my hand, she looked at the shelves I had fastened to the walls, she looked at my father's books, she took down three, four, she glanced through them, her hand opened three, four times and the books dropped onto the floor, then she said: "A lot of shit."

After saying that word, she took my hands again, but this time Virginie pushed me along, we went back into her room where she began undressing. Her coat, which she unhooked, her dress which she pulled off and tossed aside and I turned my head away, when I looked at her again she was wearing a dressing gown, she was silent, she had removed her make-up.

Stretched out on the bed beside her, I recounted to her, at her request, my first days at school. It was too short on account for her taste and she started asking me questions. Was I getting on all right? I told her that everything was going well, yes, I liked the masters, no they didn't question me, there were so many of us, no I hadn't any friends, they didn't appeal to me. She for her part thought that I ought to make friends, that I should not always give the impression of being somewhere else, or rather—Virginie corrected herself—of thinking of something else. I promised my sister.

And how many times had my father come? I

was used to Virginie saying "your father" when speaking of ours and all that surprised me was the question. She knew perfectly well seeing that she had been at home with him. Virginie repeated her question, I said three times, she thought that was a lot.

She dressed and made up, all in the twinkling of an eye. I looked out of the window at the street. Virginie wanted me to take her out to dinner. The idea appealed to me. She stuffed bank notes into a new purse which she gave me informing me that from now on it was I who would handle our money, like that I would have to think of the rent, the outings, I would be the person in charge. . . . People looked at her a great deal and at me too out of the corners of their eyes, as if she were not my sister. Virginie seemed pleased to have these men's and women's eyes lingering on her and twice she told me that I counted for very little in the sight we offered. Indeed, for nothing. So as not to hurt me perhaps, she also assured me twice that, if I wished, I could have my turn at being noticed. I would have to make certain efforts, about which she promised to speak to me, when the moment was ripe. I said nothing, I thought nothing of Virginie's remarks, her beauty overawed me.

She chose the meal for us both. She made me

recite the list of dishes we were going to have. It was I who would speak to the headwaiter. She insisted on a strong drink to begin with. Virginie emptied her glass at a gulp and, when I had finished mine, she wanted another. I said no but Virginie probably disliked drinking by herself and I had to order another two glasses. This time my sister took her time emptying her glass, I wondered why, I noticed that the waiters were getting impatient. I started dreaming, dozing. I had had a second helping of every course. Virginie got up so abruptly that I jumped.

My father made the journey six times between the 5th of October and the 5th of November. Virginie gave me these figures, irritated. She kept going away, coming back, her classes did not begin until the 15th of November. She came back smiling one morning, she had had a long talk with my father about me, it had been decided that he would come less often, Virginie had explained to him that I had to get used to our new life and work hard, things from which, according to her, visits distracted me. Virginie had lied. I hurled furious reproaches at her. I think she was expecting that reaction. She came up to me, her hand ran lightly over my face, she said to me father, Indiana, they are getting old and traveling tires them so much, both of them, I lied for their sake, for our sake. That evening we talked a great deal about our father, about Indiana, Virginie was gentle and affectionate her hand went on stroking and now and then I heard: "It's all over . . . it's finished. . . . Don't think about it any more . . .," as people say to children when they cry.

On the 5th of November, I remember that date too because I was not to see him again until the Christmas holidays, on the 5th of November my father came back. He brought me a bulky book on the Canadian Indians which he left with me, without having read it himself. On the terrace in front of the station I lingered with Indiana. I looked at her hair, her eyes, I uncovered her teeth. Then, with my father, we went for a drive far out along the Avignon road, as if we were not coming back. And it is true that I came back alone. My father was silent, I could feel that he was thinking of turning back, I kissed him, I jumped out of the buggy, I stopped the bus I had seen coming toward us and I ran after it while it was slowing down and stopping, I fled from the buggy like a thief. I went on writing to him as often as before and twice, three times a week I sent a package. He did the same.

With her classes starting the following week, Virginie put a stop to her coming and going. I remember that on her last trip she brought back, apart from a few books, an extraordinary wardrobe which she unpacked in front of me for she wanted me to admire everything with her and, so she told me, never to criticize. Dresses, skirts, costumes, jumpers and I was pleased not to know exactly how to tell the difference between a suit and a two-piece, I liked these new words. Virginie stroked the finest materials for a long time and held them out at arm's length, holding her breath, so that I should wax enthusiastic with her and my sister said: "I shall wear that one for three months . . . that one for five years" and, once, she went up to a century. My heart beat wildly for that long promise. But Virginie was versatile. She was constantly changing her clothes and I never saw her put on anything which she had worn three times. She liked for a few hours what she had promised to like for eternity.

The morning after this return, which I can describe so to speak as final, Virginie asked me the questions I had already heard: Was I getting on all right? Yes, everything was going well. The masters? They did not question me much, there were so many of us. Had I made any friends? No. Virginie lost her temper again at that point. She told me of ways of approaching them, she said:

"Dodges." Virginie thought too that I ought to keep quiet about my knowledge of Indian languages. In the first place, nobody would believe me. But if I were found to be telling the truth, how could I avoid being labeled with such ridiculous, shameful nicknames as the Indian, the Virginian, the M.D. boy? I rather liked the first two, I did not quite grasp the meaning of the third. I smiled and perhaps she guessed that I was going off into a dream. Her insults shook me out of it, an unfamiliar litany in which I recognized only the one word "shit" and I hated Virginie for using it so freely.

Before her anger had really cooled she was on her feet, ready to go out. I followed her. A few minutes later, however surprising I found Virginie's behavior, I had forgotten my distress: she knew everybody. Boys and girls of about her age, but some older, especially among the boys, shook hands with her, kissed her. They finally noticed me and asked, or implied with a jerk of the head: "Who's he?" And Virginie replied: "He's my brother." A handshake and their attention returned to Virginie. Others asked no questions, but she said: "My brother." One boy tapped her stomach, a second put his arm around her, stroked her waist. Yes, she had gotten a little thinner, they laughed heartily. A third ran his fingers around Virginie's breasts. She fluttered her eyelashes. Nobody was embarrassed by my presence.

We went up and down a street several times like that, Virginie and I, never alone, Virginie chatting away, I saying nothing. When the two of us were finally back in her room I asked her about those boys. I was thinking of the one who had tapped her stomach and the other, the boy who had fingered her breasts. She told me: "Pals." She added that they were mine too and that we would be seeing them often, when we felt like it and they felt like it too.

Then she wanted us to go to the movies. Were my classes that afternoon important? I thought they were. Virginie assured me they were not. We went out again. I had decided, without thinking about my sister, to go to the movies twice a week. She gave an irritated laugh when I told her. I think she disliked my deciding things, planning, arranging, unpriming them. She reveled in surprises, impulsive actions, whims, caprices, prolonged shilly-shallying, she would say yes, then no, yes again, and no, time with her was always trembling at the end of her line, appearing, disappearing, re-appearing, it went under like a fisherman's float and bobbed up again, invariably, and I used to think that if Virginia had left it alone time would have died but she teased it with a knife and showed me the Cain's eye of its texture, while I for my part tried to turn all the things which are life and which wear away the heart: events, incidents, into still, sleepy little pebbles, in the depths of my memory where my quicksands and forgetful beaches lie.

I spoke about Westerns and said that I did not want to miss them, provided they were in color. I ought not to bother with them any more, in her opinion, they belonged to a period of my life which was over. I resolved to go by myself to the movie houses where they were showing and to say nothing about this except to my father.

Apart from the fact that Virginie was ready to see anything but Westerns, I might have imagined myself back in the past. Thus, once, we went to the movies every night for a whole week. Some time after that, we saw three films in one day. Virginie used to discuss them late at night, in her room, with her friends, "the gang" she called them and I never managed to count the gang, some nights it consisted of a score of boys and girls, three or four on other nights. There were people coming, going, coming back and I was curious about the reason for this ebb and flow about which Virginie was unconcerned, which she did not even see for

I would ask her: "Why don't we see anything more of the tall fair-haired chap with the goatee?" and Virginie, after a moment's thought, would reply: "That's true, he's disappeared." Then she would go on to something else.

It was a good thing that she had a schedule at the University which kept her at lectures and classes, during the first four days of the week, until seven o'clock in the evening. I was able to work for hours at a stretch. I needed to feel time in front of me whereas Virginie varied between laziness and frenzy, she was capable of working for three days on end, without changing out of her dressing gown, almost without sleeping, almost without eating, at those times she would close her door to everyone and sometimes Virginie went for weeks without opening a book, she knocked mine about, deliberately lost the pages I marked, the slips of paper I put in my books, she had invented a game which I did not dare to interrupt, for fear that she might go further in her enthusiasm: butterflies. Virginie would throw into the air, ten or twenty at a time, my white sheets of paper, and the game was that they should come close to the ceiling without touching it for they would have fallen too heavily and, when Virginie succeeded, the sheets of paper fluttered to the floor, in pairs, in threes or fours, all

mixed up and I would say, just like her: "Look, big
tired butterflies." I would bend down, she would
cry: "Leave them." I got into the habit of number-
ing the sheets of paper on which I wrote my exercises for school and those which I intended for
my father, in foreign languages. On the same sheets
of paper I also copied out beautiful phrases.

At Christmas of that year when it was so hot
and the 1st of October saw my admission to the
lycée, we went back home. I had no difficulty in
believing Virginie when she told me that she was
coming just for my sake, to keep me company.
What she would have liked was for us to stay here,
the two of us, and above all, after three months
at Montpellier, for me to have lost the desire to go
back to the village. Not that I was pining for my
father. If I thought about our separation, I felt
that, far away from him in this town, I was with
him at home. Virginie tried in all sorts of ways,
when the gang met in her room, to interest me in
their conversation. I was pleased, nothing more,
that she attached some importance to my feelings,
my opinions but I felt embarrassed when she insisted, I would have liked her to take me into
account in private, something she rarely did, being
too interested in herself I think. I answered people
after a fashion. She made me try the wine every-

body drank, which the boys brought along. It was a long time before I noticed that couples kept slipping away and going into my room. Virginie's friends were tidy people who left no trace of their visits and they were so uninterested in the Indians, in Virginia about 1842, that they never touched my books. I would have noticed the marks made by their fingers. I think that it was because my blindness touched her that Virginie, one evening, told me to go into my room to "see what they were doing." The couple had fallen asleep. I did not wake them up. Virginie had to knock on the wall. From that moment on, I could feel that she was worried, impatient for the gang to go, she kept looking at me more than usual. When we were alone, and the glasses washed, the room tidied up, she followed my example and picked up a book. But her curiosity, or her anxiety, overcame her desire to hear me speak first. What was I thinking about? I hesitated, I was remembering my room in darkness, the boy and the girl a single body, I was wondering if they were all like that, if there might not be some who would steal my books. I did not dare to express my fears and Virginie thought I was shocked. She said: "That's only natural. You'll do the same." I left her, her smile, that evening, was unbearable.

On other occasions, when we were alone together, she was irritated by my absentmindedness.
She told me that I would never change and I replied quickly, so that she could not hear me properly, that I was happy at the thought of staying the
same, always. Then it was "shit" all the time, until
I went back to my room then she came in, as I
have read that mothers do when their children are
asleep, but I was not yet asleep and, as she bent
over me, I heard: "Good boy . . . little shit," then
Virginie tiptoed out of the room.

Our journey, by bus, was uneventful. I did not
feel sick and I told myself that presumably, without my knowing it, I had grown tougher. We went
as far as Avignon, where my father was waiting
with Indiana. I knew that he would be there, he
had written to tell me so and I had taken care not
to inform Virginie. She recognized the buggy some
way off, her cheeks flushed. I was afraid, at that
moment, that her anger was going to explode in
front of everybody, but my sister kept it in check,
an effort which made her even more beautiful than
usual, between pink and red.

Our habits reclaimed us. Virginie did not leave
her room, except to join us at mealtimes, but she
appeared in the middle and even at the end of

the readings. My father did not look up. The first day, at the first reading, I saw his hand, it was trembling slightly and, in spite of the bookmark, he did not open the book right away at the correct page. His voice rose, a little hoarse at first and as it were unsteady, searching for something which may have been the voice, the intonation of the past but he found them, after a few lines: he had chosen some pages from the second part of the account which Clark and Lewis wrote of the expedition they undertook in 1804, to reach the Pacific coast in Oregon by land and by the Missouri, in the heart of the Sioux country. This second part related their return journey. Clark, Lewis, my father, in phrases which were simplicity itself, described the joy which travelers feel, after a long absence, when they return to their country, their village, their house and they also described how in those who go away and come back there is a great deal of the prodigal son so that the others, who have stayed at home and welcome them back, are clumsy in finding words of love. Even Virginie listened.

And in the morning I stayed in my room, I could hear Virginie in hers, I wanted to reproach her for arriving late at the readings, for staying away but her face, when I met her, was hard. I suffered from

this attitude and in the afternoon, when my father
came in from the estate and found me in his office,
I kept thinking too much about Virginie to be
really alone with him as we had been in the past,
long ago it seemed to me, for the pages of their
story were so powerful that I confused my three
months at Montpellier with the two and a half
years Lewis and Clark were away and my father
felt something, a certain constraint, perhaps a certain aloofness, he said scarcely anything to me and
at times when I had my head bent over my books
and my writing, I could feel his gaze. I did not look
up, so that he would not have to turn his face away.
In the evening in my room, I examined my con-
science, I examined his, if something had broken,
it was not in him, not in me, it was, how shall I
put it, between us. Sitting opposite him in the office
my thoughts took me back to Montpellier and I
remembered the gang, those boys, those girls, and
the evenings, our walks, Virginie's ways. Regretting
that she was not like us, in harmony with us, I
regretted not being like her and found it odd, when
I came to think of it, that at Montpellier it was as
if I had not left home whereas I felt, here, that I
had left Montpellier.

I came back to the subject of Queshuan, I told
my father how enthusiastic I was to learn it, from

him, with him, that I had found a new grammar on the shelves but he shook his head, then said: "Who would correct your exercises, the first ones, which are always so difficult and require me to be with you?" I thought immediately of that promise we had made to each other, of that line of conduct which we had fixed together, on the spur of the moment, according to which I was to come home every Wednesday, every Saturday night, I had forgotten. My father spoke fast, he understood, he knew how difficult it was, we were far apart, yes too far away from each other, we would never have been able to arrange things satisfactorily and if I had kept my promise, I would have spent the time in trains, in buses, in the buggy too and I would have been unable to do any serious work so that I was wise to give up Queshuan, a language which in any case, according to my father, was not a real language of the real South, but that of the extreme, exaggerated South, where it was far too hot.

We set off again, Virginie and I, my father drove us by night, with Indiana and we took the train at Avignon. Right up to our arrival Virginie sat stiffly on the seat, silent and my attempts to re-ingratiate myself provoked threatening gestures. On the platform, however, she changed, once again I found her volatile, unpredictable. Then as we were walking to our rooms, Virginie opened her mouth once to tell me that she had an idea.

My sister saying no more on the subject, that day and the following days, I forgot to ask her about the idea. Virginie had changed again but I found too many advantages in her new behavior to risk any remarks. She let me go to my room and no longer insisted on my staying with her until the evening. From now on my sister undressed alone. Since the wall was too thick for me to hear her, I imagined the padding of her bare feet, the rumpling of her clothes, the rasping murmur when Virginie slips her body between the sheets and I saw on the sheets her nightdress rising and falling on a level with her breasts, I listened to her breathing inside me, I disappeared inside her. Then, my imagination tiring, the pictures growing dim, I immersed myself in my books, deep in those from school, deeper still in my father's.

She picked a thundering quarrel with me. The first thing was that I had promised her, for the sake of peace and quiet, that in January I would approach three or four boys in my class and invite them to our rooms: by this means Virginie had no doubt that I would make some friends. I had forgotten, January had gone by. She would also have liked me to go out alone and she often described to me the town at night, its lights, its mysteries, the chance meetings, the faces glimpsed between light and shade. I found it hard to picture these things, incapable as I was of expressing them.

That evening I am talking about, Virginie, beside herself with fury, was so close to me, her head almost touching mine, that I allowed my eyes to be trapped by the heaving of her breasts and I thought, dreamed that I was there, at that place in her body, the source of her anger. Her chest contracted, I had warning of the insults before they struck me, then when Virginie drew breath I tried to explain to her what I was like and the scene lasted while her breasts rose and fell a hundred times, I told Virginie of my hatred of walks, of walkers, of strolls and strollers, that way living creatures have of surrendering themselves to the sunshine, to the warmth, sometimes it is to the softness of the air, to the stillness of things, meanwhile time goes by they notice nothing, it is already evening, another day, they are a little less alive, dead a little more, one day nearer their end and I told Virginie of my hatred of the mind when it surrenders itself like that, all calm and tranquil, for two pins, with the day dragging on indefinitely, it would believe in eternity, when it is already 1843, 1892, 1952, 1958 and still we go on so that

Virginia seems to be receding, for all that it is firmly anchored and waiting in 1842 and Virginie I finally reduced to silence, I saw her breasts become still and I thought that she was listening to me, she too, that perhaps my words had fixed her, living and motionless, for all eternity, then Virginie turned her head away, concealing her breasts from me.

My sister took a few steps toward the window then she came back toward me, a sort of gentle anxiety in her, caressingly she said "little shit," didn't I know that we all have to die, one day, besides I mustn't think about it but live along with time, in harmony with time, inside it, I must force myself to grow up, allow myself to grow old and I interrupted her, shaking my head: "Exactly . . . Exactly . . .," whereas for Virginie those two movements seemed to be distinct, she went on: "You must live your life" and I translated: "You must die your death." Virginie told me what other people were like and how to use things, she talked about girls, women, tarts, passion, drink and gambling, she prayed to all the gods that I should drink myself to death, to death she said with a laugh, she described scenes of orgy to me and the revelation, splendid at first, then crushing, of bodies when they are stripped and I said: "Exactly . . . Exactly . . .," it seemed to me that I knew everything without having experienced anything and perhaps the knowledge of everything lies in the awareness of time passing but Virginie would not give up her point, she wanted me to be swamped with girls and riddled with debts, I'll pay them she said, laughing, for Virginie life seemed a step toward death and that step is taken back, suspended, life an incessant, imperceptible regression as if Virginia were thirty, twenty seconds away but in the end it reached the point where I was waiting for it, the fifties and even the forties, she told me of the woman, the only one or almost the only one, the children, the resigned feeling of decline and I revolted, I cried: "Resigned! . . . Resigned! . . . ," Virginie flew into a temper and said idiot, did I think I could change the world?

Exhausted, we talked about this and that and I imagined myself already alone with *The Essential History of Florida Situated in the West Indies,* by Laudonnière, which I had just received in a package from my father, between her room and mine Virginie, who followed me, had passed from anger to friendly excitement. I noticed that her eyes were shining, her hands impatient, she took a seat facing me after I had sat down at the table and, bending forward, whispering, she reminded me that she had had an idea at the end of our last journey, and if she had concealed it then it was in order to examine it, judge it, brood over it, give more weight to it from one hour to the next for Virginie never had any doubts that it was a good idea, namely: that I should write a book. Seeing that I was so fond of them! I promptly saw myself back at home, I lived the scene: my father, every day at mealtimes, reading three, four pages of my book, *The Journey to Virginia*, long, endless sentences in which the commas were hooks on which to strangle time, I described the scene to Virginie but the book, in her opinion, ought not to tell of my father, Virginia, myself as I saw us, she regarded it as a means, for me, of breaking away, of putting to sea as it were, a way of changing. I saw *The Journey to Virginia* as a book in which to bury myself. She thought of the book as a journey into the unknown. True, I would put myself into it as I was but, when the last page had been written, I would no longer be the person I had been. Who, then? Virginie did not know exactly but said that she was sure that she was right.

"You'll tell of our life, yours above all, you'll describe your father, you'll expose the old, idiotic, ancestral oak side of his character, for instance what he told us one day, that he would have liked to have another daughter, and if she had been born he would have called her, just think of it, Mary-Land or Marie-Land. . . ."

"No, I don't think that I'll put it that way. . . ."

"And at Mass on Sundays, we would go into church, your father first, then our mother, then me, then you, and finally the maidservant bringing up the rear. . . ."

"No, I don't see it in the same way as you, and besides, what interest have those details?"

"And the parish priest whom you didn't like. . . ."

"That's true, I don't like him. . . ."

"And you'll describe the heat, the wind, the *corridas*, the bullfights at Nîmes which your father never allowed us to attend and also the tramps who almost had regular dates for passing through our villages, about every three months, they were like distant relatives people felt ashamed of, but picturesque, living on tomatoes and the grapes people gave them and when they miss a season there is always somebody who remembers them, saying: 'Jean must have kicked off the old boozer' and everybody starts imagining a lonely, miserable death beside a deserted road in winter, with the rucksack, the empty bottles. . . ."

"Yes, yes, that's all very interesting, but it seems to me that those stories won't have any place in my book. . . ."

"You're wrong. They will. Because you liked them those dirty ragged tramps, and the gypsies too, you used to run to meet them. . . ."

"Yes, I liked them, but all the same that's no reason. . . ."

"Remember there was one man, I've forgotten his first name, or his surname, he had a woman with him, who was still young when we first saw her and almost beautiful, but she drank, like him, and every time they came she had grown older, uglier, she stank. . . ."

"Yes, yes, I remember. . . ."

"Besides, we never saw her twice with the same man, she went with three tramps and changed partners from one season to the next. . . ."

"Yes, I remember, but I don't see any point in describing those things in my book. . . ."

"And you'll write about the traveling knife grinders, all that, the tramps, the gypsies and so on is typical of our part of the world, you know, the knife grinders with their little carts, their odds and ends, the grindstone and the little tank full of water, how you used to look at them, for hours on end, the knives scraping against the grindstone made people run a mile but you, you went on looking. You'll write about them. . . ."

"Maybe, maybe, but I didn't think about them just now when you gave me the idea of writing this book, the urge to write it and even now. . . ."

"You're wrong. You're an idiot. It's full of poetry, all that. And you'll write about the flocks of sheep, that never-ending procession past the door, I remember you wanted to become a shepherd, you used to prowl around them. . . ."

"I don't know, I can't see how I can put sheep in my book, perhaps one or two, or a whole flock once. . . ."

"You see, I'm writing your book for you. And you'll come back to your father, of course, it's true that he played an important part and I'm thinking of some chapters in which you settle his hash, so to speak, for instance you say that he has always refused to have a telephone and that when his clients wanted to see him on business they had to come in person, they had to call at the office to ask for an appointment and, when the appointment had been made for the following morning, the peasants went home only to come back again, wasting precious time when it would have been so simple to phone, so logical too and you'll mention the long faces the peasants pulled, you'll say too that your father was, without the slightest doubt, the best solicitor in the district, which explains. . . ."

"Yes, I'll say that my father was the best solicitor, but as for his clients pulling long faces, you're making that up it seems to me, I've never noticed it. . . ."

"That's because you don't see things. I saw that fault in you from your way of speaking, you cheat with words, you make them say dreams, lies, you love them only for themselves. I'll help you, you'll describe the fairs in the villages in summer, the merry-go-rounds, the dances, your books will be full of true stories, the sort that happen every day, your readers won't feel lost, out of their depth. . . ."

"Perhaps. Perhaps I shall write what you have told me about the tramps who almost have regular dates for passing, human clocks so to speak and perhaps the villagers, by means of those vagabonds, become aware of time, now and then every three months and I imagine that if they take such cruel pleasure in picturing the death agony of the tramps, it is not so much that they are pleased about their death as about the death of the time which the tramps, every three months. . . ."

"You're talking rubbish. If you start writing like

that, you'll never finish your book. And nobody will understand a word of it either. But that diatribe of yours has made me think of something: you must write in short sentences. . . ."

"But you yourself. . . ."

"Yes," said Virginie, "I know, I've just been talking in long sentences, but I was excited by this idea of the book, I lost my head whereas you'll keep yours, you'll write your book as soberly as a man."

I set to work. The night of the idea we talked a lot more, far into the morning, Virginie precisely, I evasively when I had to answer her and my sister went on repeating tirelessly that my book would be in short sentences, she quoted precedents to me, great names, famous works, then she drew stories and people from her memory and sure enough I had lived the former, known the latter, I recognized the whole of that world and discovered that, on the fringe of my life in Virginia about 1842, I had led an earthbound existence which had slipped inside me, without jolting me, without awakening me and now that my sister was sharing her memories with me, I had to admit that I had some, I interrupted her unhappily: "So many memories, already," I could feel that my memory was heavily laden, unknown to me and at my cost the treacherous mechanism was recording life as it is, aging and mortal.

I told her: "No, I shall write my book alone, I shall not ask you for anything." Virginie agreed, on condition that she had a right of inspection. But when, at what point in the book? I decided that I would keep her informed about my progress, my difficulties and I promised to show her the pages which satisfied me. Virginie said good but if by any chance about page thirty I was not pleased with it, I would let her read it all the same. Yes. Weariness was not weighing on her eyes whereas I could scarcely keep mine open. She guessed that I wanted to be alone. It was dawn. Lying in my room, I summoned a sleep that was prompt and dreamless but the idea of the book kept me awake, I suddenly felt miserable and lonely, with no strength or courage, so I paddled motionless toward my pictures and, with the current soon carrying me along, I saw myself as John Smith when he went off, his people behind him, and behind me there were pages written and rustling, along the roads of Ohio, across New York, Missouri, Illinois, I traveled toward the Promised Land.

I wrote to my father: "I am writing a book."

Having mailed my letter one Monday, I watched for the postman that Wednesday morning when my classes at school started late and Indiana turned the corner of the street. I wanted to tell Virginie but, at her door, something prevented me from going in, besides my father was already coming upstairs. As we were going into my room, I heard the sound of a bolt, Virginie was shutting herself in. She must have gone out a little later.

I questioned him, as I usually did, about the house, the estate, the animals, the books and he for his part asked if everything was going well, the classes, the exercises and compositions in Indian languages, which he would correct later on, when I had set off for school. I was burning to hear him talk about the book. He did not ask about it, so had he received my letter? Early in the afternoon, when we had finished the meal he had cooked and we had eaten facing one another, Virginie still giving no sign of life, he waved his arm in a sweeping gesture which took in all the books on the shelves and he asked if they would be in it. I said that yes, I was thinking of including them. And him? Him too. Me? The estate? Virginia? Virginie? I said yes, everyone, every one of us.

He smiled. I wondered if he were going to ask me any other questions, if, like Virginie a few days earlier, he would try to extract promises from me, for instance that I should give him thirty pages of the manuscript to read. The conversation turned to other subjects and I sensed that my father was not going to return to the book. Then, before he left, as he was getting ready, I told him that he would be the first to read the novel from end to end, not a chapter here and there, but everything, all at one time. He replied: "I trust you" and his hand moved backward and forward over the spines of the volumes lined up in the room. He could have taken some away, he was too fond of the packages I sent him.

Virginie appeared much later. I realized that she regarded my father's visit as null and void. I was sitting at my table, writing, she went straight into her room. On the landing however she said something which I half-heard and which may have been, but I cannot be sure, "Don't allow yourself to be distracted" or "Don't allow yourself to be recaptured." It is the last word which is missing.

She behaved, during the first days after the idea, with considerable tact and discretion, an attitude which I think was an effort for her. For Virginie a book to be written was too novel an idea for her to have any clear-cut ideas on its execution. For example, my sister, for a moment, wanted me to work as she worked, in other words under the impetus of inspiration. She kept repeating the word "inspiration." It appealed to her. A little later, she modestly recognized that it befitted my book better than her studies. But what advice was she to give me? While reserving the right to intervene, after fifty pages, Virginie left me free to write the first pages as I thought fit. So that I was able, by myself, to come to an arrangement with time and I divided it in this way: in the morning, I would get up an hour earlier, namely at five o'clock and, after a quick wash, work on the book until seven; then a more thorough wash, and I expected the soap and water to efface, until nine o'clock in the evening when I would start work on the book again, all weariness, doubts, anxiety; in the meantime, school. That finished at four o'clock. I allowed myself an hour's relaxation. And from five o'clock till seven, when we had dinner, work on my exercises for school and the Indian languages. I allotted myself six hours of sleep, a little more on Saturday and Sunday when, with no school, I planned to divide my time in practically equal parts: for homework, the book, the languages.

I wrote out this timetable and Virginie read it. She was neither for nor against: we would see. She remarked that I handled figures well and that

I seemed, at present, to be taking an interest in the clock. I had surprised myself, a little earlier. For a long time I had thought that, to prevent time from moving on, it was necessary to pull it back. I now discovered that it does not move on either if it is foreshadowed. Then it jumps backward. The future is abolished at one stroke, five years, eleven centuries, more, all the time one wants, it promptly becomes time past. For example, as soon as Virginie had given me the idea of the book, without knowing how I was going to begin I wrote, right at the bottom of a sheet of paper, the last sentence. My book, I believe, will not surprise me, its conclusion is already in Virginia.

Little by little, the day joined in. I had such a start on it about January and February that if for a wonder I had been able to imagine it, for two or three seconds, I would have come to the conclusion that it would never catch up with me. However, invisible, it was to begin nibbling away. Once, when I got up, it had risen before me. Virginie gave way, without really understanding, I had the curtains I wanted, thick, deep, they annulled the sun.

My sister, at first, in order to encourage me, because she imagined that I would like to feel her, active, a few feet away, also set her alarm clock for five. But she fidgeted and moved around too much. What is more, she came into my room for no good reason, she had really thought I was calling her, a shout in the street probably, she would have sworn it came from my room or was her handkerchief here, which she had been looking for for nearly an hour? I told Virginie not to appear in the morning before breakfast. She obeyed. She must have missed the glances she used to dart at my papers. Virginie, I realize now, did not hate receiving my orders: they came from me. So she chose to sleep, her beauty, moreover, benefited as a result. Not that she granted me unreserved confidence and I think that there was some mistrust mingled with her affection and her curiosity. Thus I would hear her so to speak muffling her footsteps: she would emerge from her room, approach my door and not come in. She must have listened to hear if the pen was scratching and looked at me through the keyhole. Then she would go back to bed.

I used to wake her then for breakfast. Not once did Virginie complain about that secondary condition I was in about seven o'clock when, far from my book but still in my book, incompletely roused and recovered from it, I bumped into the door and the furniture, I walked with a heavy, clumsy step

Virginie jumped, startled out of her sleep. On the contrary, she was full of affection right away, she pressed me to her and, gripping my arms, she bent them around her waist, she mimed a rolling motion in the bed so that as my arm went up, her breasts leaped over my wrists, into my hands and Virginia said: "Squeeze, squeeze," I closed my hands and Virginie said: "You are changing, you are growing up." I tried to make her talk about anything except the book. But already at breakfast and again at midday when I rejoined her, at any and every moment of the day, of the evening, she indulged in a running fire of questions. How was it going? How many pages? What was in it? The tramps, the fairs, the sheep? Oh, no, they weren't in it, they might be later. Father, herself? Yes, they were beginning to appear. How? She really must wait, I couldn't tell her right off, sum up, solidify what I was spreading out, decomposing. Virginie quite understood. She said good, you are probably right. Then she returned to the attack.

Meanwhile Virginie attributed to the book an influence of which she thought that out of playfulness, or modesty, I was concealing most of the effects. She joked about it and claimed, this was the word she used, to be "uncovering" me. My sister did not really believe that I was just as bored as before at the gang's meetings in her room, those endless discussions about nothing in particular and everything under the sun, I noticed that the gang's intelligence and language were no subtler as a result, they used up time, forced it to pass. As for the flirtations, the assignations in my room, using my new authority, citing the book as a pretext, I finally got my sister to forbid them and to lock my door. Preoccupied as she was with me, did Virginie notice that she was changing slightly? I could not get used to all the drinking either. Virginie would have liked us to move. Once she said to me: "A new room, just one room for us both, but a huge one and we shall be closer to one another while retaining the necessary independence, for instance we shall put our working tables at opposite ends of the room." I said no. She insisted. I rebelled. Virginie gave way: "It doesn't really matter, you are right, other things are more important."

More serious and indeed grave, then alarming, in her eyes was the fact that I still did not go out alone. Perhaps her eye, pressed to the keyhole sometimes in the mornings, looked for me in the hope of not finding me. Virginie spoke in a somewhat hoarse, irritating voice and a shiver went down my spine when, in spite of myself, I listened to her say: "I would like you to be secretive, with lots of mysteries, adventures, vices and sensing all that, then uncovering it, I would enjoy a great, sweet happiness." She had bought several bottles of some English or American liquor, which she said she was mad about, something I found hard to understand as it tasted like medicine and every evening, every midday, before sitting down to table, Virginie offered me a glass. Noticing my disgust, she said that I would get into the habit. I wanted no habits.

Virginie tried to give a new direction to my reading. She pretended not to see my father's packages and she was not there when I was preparing those I was going to send him, an operation on which I expended time and care, I was so terrified that the package might come undone, that the books might be lost or damaged. Virginie had her own books and I had to read several of them before concluding that she must be affecting or exaggerating some of the violent feelings which she displayed about them. But she showed skill and a sort of art in awakening my interest, then unleashing it. She set off calmly in search of descriptions, evocations, a journey which I thought would go straight to the heart of the book and without knowing it I was already there, I was imagining landscapes, rides, girls and Virginie had pronounced all those words, but she had not reached the point where, restraining my impatience, I was waiting for her to clarify and nourish my visions, she had turned off somewhere and along winding lanes her whispering voice told of riders careless of their mounts, eager to hand them over to their servants and I asked: "Why? Why?" then these characters came together, sometimes a couple, often several, they strolled through gardens laid out in the French style, in the English style, they supped of choice dishes and, toward the end of the meal, Virginie's voice became reticent, distant, almost muffled, it seemed to be emerging from the veils and stoles which the ladies in her story had discarded, or which had been torn from them and though no longer asking: "Why? Why?" I begged her to make herself clear, to go on to the end, to tell me everything, but Virginie said: "It isn't really your sort of book. But you can read it if you like."

She did not give it to me, she had lent it, or lost it, it would be returned to her, she would find it again, that was certain, a promise. Days went by, I had almost forgotten the book, I found it on my table next to mine and a work on the Indians, open. Virginie's scandalous books set my blood on fire. Yet I considered them extremely monotonous and that is why I think that my sister exaggerated the admiration she felt for them. She flaunted her influence over me, her eclectic culture, I did not realize that her superiority lay in the three years which make Virginie my elder. Nowadays I sometimes find myself murmuring under my breath, just to myself: "Old Virginie, old Virginie." I also tell myself that I shall never catch up with her and that perhaps I shall never catch her age, her disease. Where I live, in Virginia about 1842, nothing of what I confide to myself surprises me and, often, I convince myself. If I had known how at that time, I would have escaped from my sister and the fascination of her books: they showed that one can also die of pleasure.

She had an urge to take me to see some undressing shows which were put on in the local nightclubs. Virginie always took the initiative in going out when, tired out, I was emerging from my work and felt a longing to relax, to set off anywhere and do anything. I wanted a cat and I would have spent hours stroking it, on my bed, until the courage to work returned to me. Virginie hated cats. The first time, at a nightclub, she had the impression that we were being taken in. The second time, at another, she admitted that she had been mistaken as to the very nature of the show. There was no more talk of nightclubs.

Then Virginie asked herself: "Why didn't I think

of it earlier?" She was thinking of Nature. There again I had to follow her. It was no use my reminding her of the demands of my timetable. Virginie said that I would work all the more and all the better for breathing some fresh air. We went out early, on foot. Virginie said: "Look, learn to see, observe, for the sake of your book" and I remembered how I had loved the fields, the woods, not very long ago and yet that passion seemed childish to me now. She put things as it were under my nose and, rightly deciding that they were beautiful, I went into endless ecstacies over them. I remember some almond trees in blossom, they were standing along the edge of a large estate like frivolous sentries, an inducement to trespass and trespass I did, following Virginie who ran along in a transport of delight, but for some time the shrubs had been visible on our right and Virginie had been waiting for me to see them, we were going to pass them, I behaving as if they did not exist, they were going to disappear, Virginie pointed them out to me in a fury. We went up to each almond tree, running our fingers over the trunks and admiring the flowers, the heavy branches. Virginie, how could I forget it, said lightly and playfully: "This is like Virginia, isn't it?" I said no, all of a sudden I hated those trees.

All the same, I forgave my sister. Indeed it was

I who later reminded her of the almond trees, of those at least for she must have found others. She saw beautiful things so clearly, she saw so many of them and no doubt there are so many to see, that in the end she mixed them up, forgot them, each new marvel evicting its predecessor. Often I felt sorry for her, for Virginie, the world for her is so full of almond trees of all sorts and great beauty that she does not need to remember them, still less imagine them. She is incapable of anything but seeing. I feel sure that she has never had trees which have sprung up by themselves within her, sprung from nothing, sprung from words, from the earth her blood.

We had to give up our Sunday outings, we were never alone, thousands of people and more were doing the same as we—or else it was we who were doing the same as they. Virginie said Saturday— and we met the same crowds. So we walked ever farther and Virginie was delighted at not knowing where—or when we should be going home. She had to change her tune. Out there too, several miles from Montpellier, in the heart of the woods and the underwoods, up on the hills and down the fields, there were crowds of townspeople and I reflected that nobody could say "out-of-the-way places" any more. We passed lines of cars, moving along the roads, stationary in the meadows and even in the ditches, we trampled pieces of greasy paper underfoot and, when the wind was blowing, it plastered them against our ankles, did *we* take food along with us? If for a wonder the music from the radios had fallen silent, we would still have heard it as a result of being unable to avoid it for hours on end, and we strode along, Virginie and I full of scenes of murder, of carnage, of delightfully horrible accidents in which the people in the woods lost their lives and the cars lost everything, in the end we took nails with us, an idea of Virginie's and, vigilant and jubilant, we punctured as many tires as we could, hiding behind scanty bushes. We came upon, stepped across and often tripped over men who were asleep or dozing, each with his woman lying over him or within reach, next to the bottles, and there were others, standing up, who were playing ball, bowls, skittles, others again who were fooling around with nothing in their hands and nothing at their toes, all of them in the tainted air were trying to breath a little clean air, they had come along with that object in mind and I asked: "Virginie, in your opinion as a medical student, how many days, weeks, months perhaps, are these people gaining on their death, are their hearts resting a little, are their tissues getting younger?", it vexed me that she should have brought me out here and that I should resemble these people, although we had never lain down, my sister and I, we were mixed up with them and they would go home in the evening, happy, tired out, they had whiled away time and everywhere else on the hillsides and the hilltops, in byways and hollow ways, we came across other groups, other couples, other bodies and there were men, women, children by themselves, I kept asking: "Virginie, in your opinion, how many days are these people gaining on their death . . .", I thought of Virginia where, in 1842, life could not be estimated, could not be counted, or if it could it must have been in centuries, in millenaries: "Virginie, in your opinion . . .", she said: "Shit, idiot," I suddenly saw that there were twenty paces between us and I had to run after my sister, in the evening I was utterly exhausted.

So Virginie decided that we would go into the country on Thursdays. Too many children, in troops and groups and my sister told me: "I hate them, I'll never have any." When she met some, in a low voice but loud enough for several to hear, she would shoot a string of obscene words at them and the girls and boys would bow their heads. All the same we were more or less alone, with the wet, dirty, rusty rubbish of the previous Sunday. I jumped when Virginie jumped, I ran after her while she never stopped running, we went up and down slopes and I learned a word: *skylarking*, we slid, fell, our clothes were covered with dust or mud, our shoes sticky with clay or dung, how could we tell the difference without risking being sick, and we heard, I was going to say: in the distance, cars sounding their horns nearby. Once we found a spring. It looked unimpressive and the ground around it had been so well trodden that it was safe to assume that nothing would ever grow there. Another time, to please Virginie, who had devised a new game, I had hidden in a thicket and my eye fell on some pieces of wood bearing traces of paint. With Virginie resigned to waiting for me, I reconstructed the signboard and deciphered the words: BEWARE DEER AND WILD BOARS. No doubt a long time ago, several decades, a century perhaps, in 1842 who knows, this thicket, this region was an extension, a reflection of Virginia. My sister disputed the shape of the letters I made out. In her opinion I could not be absolutely certain about the deer and the wild boars. She told me: "You are imagining it." With my fingers I tried to rediscover for her the shape of the letters she had difficulty in seeing and my dirty fingers ended up leaving marks so that, according to Virginie, I invented the notice. She was sure that she was right. I am sure that I was.

We made our outings less frequent, Virginie refusing to drop them completely. Roughly one a month. I worked harder and better, at my studies as well as the Indian languages, the book, and I passed my examination, at school, there was only one left for me to pass, the following year, to become a student like Virginie. I remember that at that thought a light shone within me, I saw the years ahead of me, beautiful, orderly, numerous and the very evening of the day I sat for the examination, then the following evening and again the afternoon I learned of my success, I set to work again as if nothing had happened, and nothing had happened in fact, looking up from my books I saw myself as the great wave in the sea, a steamroller, the human form of perpetual motion, I saw myself as a woodcutter chopping at a tree which never falls despite the deepening cut and I went on wielding the axe, monotonously, without stopping, I saw in myself, I loved in myself a stubborn patience which was excited and feverish, Virginie came into my room and said: "Not long till the holidays." I saw my father, the house and the garden, the estate, Indiana, and in front of Virginie

who started getting impatient: "What idea has
bitten you now?" I counted on my fingers: ten and
I had to start again with six other fingers: for exactly sixteen days I had not written to my father
and I worked it out again: "You had two letters
from him, one after the other, at the beginning of
those sixteen days and since then your father, without any news from you, without any replies, has
stopped writing. Packages? No packages either,
for about twelve days and from you to him nothing,
not a single book returned." I said to Virginie:
"Leave me alone," she went out banging the door,
I started on my fingers again, the figure was correct and on the left-hand corner of the table I
saw the exercises in Indian languages. I had piled
them up there without thinking of sending them
off and therefore without thinking of him, my
father, I had forgotten him so to speak instinctively. Then I thought of the telephone he hasn't
got one, I thought of the telegraph, I ran to the
post office, I told my father LETTER FOLLOWS MUCH
LOVE, then I came back to my room and I guessed:
the book. It was the book's fault.

And in the letter I wrote to my father: "All my
letters are in the book, you will read them there."
I felt sure that he would reply I understand, I
know, my father knowing and understanding everything. His letter said no.

But as for Virginie, I wondered how she could go on waiting. I was afraid that she might take advantage of my absence, my sleep perhaps, to come into my room and read those pages which I could feel, far away from her at school or in the movies when a Western was showing, far away from me, hesitant and weak, vulnerable and malleable, I imagined my pages as the eagles on the estate without their wings. I told Virginie to be patient, that the reading would be soon, in a month's time, in two weeks, the following Sunday and she asked: "Sunday morning?" and I replied: "No, Sunday evening." The thought of these terms increased my uneasiness. So to forestall requests, a theft, a piece of trickery, to calm her impatience, I spoke to her about the book and I should have preferred total silence. I waited for her to be naked, in the evening, under one of her nine or twelve white nightdresses, with the blue ribbon which she did not pull tight above her breasts, below the lips still pink with the lipstick which she had touched up again in the afternoon and then, in the Virginie who came in, there was friendship perhaps, gentleness in any case and I hoped also a certain dreaminess, weakness, languid fervor and I said to her once:

"I've worked well today, you know, really well,

I was afraid of this passage in which I wanted to describe, in which I had to describe the estate, and evoke it rather than describe it, I feel that I have so little talent for description. . . ."

"Use short sentences."

"Yes, so little talent for description and I thought, instead of writing, instead of my writing, if my father spoke in a long dramatic monologue, progressing toward a drama that would take care of the inevitable description. . . ."

"Use short sentences, I tell you."

"Yes, yes, which would no longer be a description, while being one all the same and Virginie, I think I've pulled it off, more or less. . . ."

"Go on."

"The eagles too. The further I go, the more I rummage among my memories, the more indispensable I feel they are to my book and as for myself, it is as if I could not do without them. . . ."

"And as if you had seen them."

"Yes, but I have seen them, nearly seen them. . . ."

"Exactly, seeing and nearly seeing is all the same to you, in fact we have never seen any eagles except in cages."

"That isn't true. I remember their wings. . . ."

"That isn't true. You don't remember anything about them, you're making it all up because you would have liked them to fly in front of you but eagles don't exist, they don't exist any more, you never find them except in cages. How many times we went out, the two of us, you took me out and on the way, running along, you used to tell me of three eagles, six eagles. There have never been any on the estate. Do you say that we used to go out to see them and that we never . . ."

"No, it's an odd thing, now I come to think of it, but when I describe myself on the estate you aren't with me, I'm all alone, but perhaps I'll mention you later on, who knows, the fact remains that you are wrong about the eagles. . . ."

"A pure fabrication. I too have often wondered where they went, once the cage was opened. Well, they went back home to the mountains and the odds are that the sportsmen on the way never saw them again. . . . Remember the stuffed eagles nailed up in the local farms."

"Yes, covered with dust, moth-eaten, moldy, shot years ago, birds which are in the family and handed down from generation to generation, and I know very well that my father's eagles didn't know the limits of the estate, but they came back to it because of the fields, the slopes, the river and not a single sportsman, knowing they were my father's eagles . . ."

"You poor kid, go on."

"The Indians too. You can't imagine how difficult it is to put Indians in a book, to describe them as you see them and not as they are, as they were I mean. . . ."

"Short sentences, learn to use short sentences."

"Yes, as they were, I mean, and if you don't borrow a few words to create local color, the Indians don't come to life. . . . But I've used only three of those words, the least I could, just what was necessary otherwise the Indians would have been Indians for children, for fun, pushing the book along; whiling away the time whereas the more I think about it the more I realize that for me they have always been a means of withdrawing, or rather of marking time where I am, like that I push the book forward and I don't go forward myself. . . ."

"Explain."

"It's difficult. You'll see."

I saw Virginie with her elbows on the table, opposite me, her hands were supporting her face and pushing it upward slightly, puckering her flesh and narrowing her eyes so that she looked as I have seen Chinese women look in pictures, and Virginie remained perfectly still, only her eyes darted about when I moved for I got up, circled around her, sat down again, what should I say and not say? Flashes went through me, whispering: tell lies, put her on a false scent, so that she feels reassured and leaves you alone, don't give in to your fear of her, if you tell her about your book you will never write it and she will prevent you from writing it—and not knowing what to do, what to think, I made hesitant gestures toward her, my fingers closed her eyelids as they used to do in our games and pulled the blue ribbon of her nightdress, then Virginie, her lips scarcely moving, said:

"Tell me about your Indians."

I said nothing.

"How do you see them? Dirty?"

"No."

"They were."

"No."

"They were."

"No. Perhaps. What difference does it make? I have never thought about dirtiness or cleanliness in connection with them but you surprise me, I have read a hundred thousand books about the Indians, not a single one described them as dirty."

"Perhaps that's because you read only what you're looking for. I looked through one of those books once and I came across two passages, six pages apart, where it said that for want of water, but also for want of a lot else besides, they didn't wash."

"For want of what?"

"Why, what makes it certain that you couldn't have lived with them, manners, culture, civilization, yes, everything you love . . ."

She repeated: everything you love and her hands swooped down upon mine, which they seized, enclosed, pressed and when she relaxed her grasp, Virginie's fingers trailed over my skin, slow, thoughtful, I said to myself: there are dreams in the tips of Virginie's fingernails. I closed my eyes. I opened them again and by way of her outstretched arms, where the veins were throbbing, I went up to her face, pausing at her breasts which were throbbing too and Virginie, like me, had closed her eyes, I could see her lashes fluttering. Then she resumed her original position, her elbows on the table, on the palms of her hands she rested her face which she turned toward me and brought so close to mine that space in the room, at that moment, was suppressed and I tried to hang on to what I knew was behind my sister, the walls continuing, the shelves continuing, and my books, a chair, a cupboard, the door above all, the door, but these things in spite of my attempts to imagine them, to love them, did not hold fast before Virginie's eyes where, between two blinks, my reeling face came and went and I heard her, my sister, in a whisper she was hissing:

"What do you call their tents, their women?"

"Wigwams, squaws, as it happens those are two of the three words. . . ."

"And the Indians in Virginia?"

"Four tribes: the Pamunkey, the Mattaponies, the Powhatan and the Chickahominies."

"Pretty words, amusing words with which to make fun of those wretched and, all things considered, rather stupid men, who have left nothing behind them but a few woodcarvings, a few masks, a few baskets, a little leather, Indians without any natural or artificial protection, your father said so. . . ."

"No."

"Your father said they died like flies when the Europeans arrived, from their diseases, from their alcohol, your Indians died like flies and your father also said that their average span of life was not more than thirty years. . . ."

"No, Virginie, no."

"And if they had had the means, the technique, they would have shown no pity, no admiration for the beauty of their country, the bison, the trees, the bears, the eagles. . . . Your father said that when they had white men's muskets in their hands they laid waste their hunting grounds with the same ferocity and stupidity as the whites showed at the same time. . . ."

"No, I wasn't there when my father said that. . . ."

"Yes, you were there, I remember, besides he often returned to the subject and he also said that their belief in eternal life in a different country from the one in which they spent their brief existence led them to love death, to provoke it with a sort of joy or resignation. . . ."

"No, Virginie, that isn't true, not those words. . . ."

"And do you see them in that country you love, Virginia, where according to your father there were never very many of them, do you see them picking cotton in the sun and dying under the lash, as often happened with . . . ?"

I remember, later on, with Virginie at Montpellier, we went to a boxing match, it was one of her ideas, one of her caprices, I had forced myself to accompany her after saying no, after an argument, a local champion was fighting a big Negro who, how could I forget this detail, had just crossed the Atlantic and the press said he was a strong contender, two or three punches and the Negro had resigned himself to the superiority of the other man who was hitting his sides, his chest, his face above all, according to Virginie the white man was trying to get at his chin, punches which, quoting the vocabulary she could hear around her, my sister called wicked—and the Negro stayed on his feet as best he could, it was obvious that he was poor in tricks, in skill or else equipped with an old, useless technique, I for my part felt that his mind was somewhere else where punches never strike home and I staggered to my bed onto which I collapsed, empty and weary, my sister had put out the lamp and through the window open to the night there rose the timid light of a streetlamp, Virginie fell on me without my hearing her approach, barefoot, and I promptly found myself at that passage in my book where I say that she spoke to me as to a weeping child: "It's all over. . . . It's finished. . . . Don't think about it any more . . . ," with Virginie whispering, panting, my hands stroked her breasts which I had so often brushed against, touched lightly, I heard my voice I was saying to myself: take your hands away—they were fumbling feverishly under the nightdress, feeling Virginie's skin down below and we began.

Then began again. Then once more. Then yet again. Then no doubt, that night, once more. Five times Virginie went into her room from which she returned with her skin cool near the stomach. I put my hands there so that they should not burn so much, and my face. Sleep took me, gave me back to Virginie, she too gave in to it, escaped from it, each of us in turn struggled against it to return to each other. I remember that we went under at the same time for a few minutes and we emerged at the same time for, I was going to say: hours. But sleep was never a match for the two of us at once and, shortly before dawn, Virginie seemed to become aware of my exhaustion, I of hers. I did not sleep when she looked as if she would sleep for a long time, I watched over her body. As a result of looking at her and imagining her as she had been a little earlier, on me, under me desire returned to me, I awoke her with caresses. Virginie helped me in the same way, she told me so.

Once I felt her giving little bites at my chest. In that vague region on the frontiers of consciousness into which fatigue had hurled me, I was floating on mists, on cotton, on something which was nothing, which was two words: *lethargy, comas*. I knew that I was smiling. Virginie must have got tired of fostering, with her bites, the sort of happiness which my face revealed to her. She sank her teeth into the flesh above my heart. I gave a cry. From the beginning, we had not exchanged a single word.

In my surprise, my pain, I pressed her head against me and rediscovered the white glow of the streetlamp which, all night, had fallen and rested on the heap of my clothes and on Virginie's nightdress.

Then the dawn effaced it. Virginie got up to draw the curtains. It was dark once more. I wanted her to put on her nightdress again. I told her so, my first words, but she said: "You." That was her first word. When I had finished, I pressed myself against Virginie and with my mouth close to her ear I asked her, so softly that my sister, as I wished, guessed rather than heard: "Tell me all the names."

And my hand began with her breasts, which were beautiful but practically devoid of mystery for me. She whispered all the names for breasts, in French, in slang, in our local dialect and she knew a few equivalents in other languages. I learned the names given to breasts by lovers, schoolboys, doctors, the indifferent, the obsessed. True, I had read or heard nearly all of them. But I wanted details, confirmation. Then my hand moved farther down. Then it turned Virginie over. I held the nightdress open. It is a wonderful vocabulary.

It seems to me that I appreciated it as it is, fragile, delicate, and also a source of great joys, of nameless ecstasies with no other names than those.

I promised myself to use it with infinite care and to choose between the words for festivals which would be festivals of passion, intelligence and sensibility. A shadow fell over me when I discovered that I did not know how to describe Virginie's body, either the upper part or the lower, in my Indian languages. My father had not taught me, my father another shadow, it fell over me, dark and sorrowful. I chased them away, both of them, by saying to Virginie I want you.

And I took her again, at the hour of the milkmen. We fell asleep at last, for good, for a long time, I did not want to see beyond our sleep.

Then it was evening. Virginie left me to get from her room the snack which was to stand us instead of a meal—and which was to last us until the following day, when perhaps it would be light.

It was light. Early in the morning we carried my clothes, my books, my things from my room into hers. Then the shelves which I fastened to our walls as I had nailed them, six months ago already, to mine. We rolled the table into her room, into our room. On the last trip I lingered on the threshold of that room in which I had worked so much, and lived so little and I would have preferred not to lock the door. Virginie joined me, she put her arm round my neck and said: "We'll turn it into a guest

143

room." I shut the door, turned the key, it seemed to me that, until that night, my eighteen years had trailed behind me, invisible, if indeed I had ever turned my head around. I could feel them now that, standing in front of the big mirror on Virginie's wardrobe, I rediscovered the places on my body where she had pressed, bitten, kissed, scratched. I was covered with red and white marks and time had not effaced them, so many marks that I forgot the others, those which die young or age badly and I told myself that every day and every night, several times a day, several times a night, Virginie would renew them. Would prolong them. Prolong: a verb I love. I called my mistress, I said to her these marks, it is as if you had pressed hard on me, as if you had bitten, kissed, scratched me once for all, once for eternity. I saw the marks in the same light as time, people think it passes, it does not pass. I fell on my knees and with my mouth I went along her legs up to her mouth. She said you are mad and I kissed my sister, who shrugged her shoulders.

We discussed what we were going to do. Stay here and spend our holidays here. Virginie thought of going for walks, for excursions around Montpellier, for a few hours, at other times a few days, but according to her, it would be madness not to spend most of our time in this huge room here where already, half-naked and so was Virginie who in the morning changed out of the nightdress she had worn that night into a new one, I was displaying a certain nonchalance. She dreamed, and I with her, of a burning, luxurious intimacy, she would buy new armchairs, bedspreads one for each day, embroidered sheets one for each night, rugs, flowers, ornaments, exotic chocolates. I was especially glad that she had thought of rugs, which would muffle even the sound of our bare feet. But the money? I said the word and for the second time my father loomed up, sitting on the buggy he was whipping Indiana, forcing her along to reach me quickly. I think that Virginie had already settled that problem. She replied I've got a plan, don't worry about the money, I'll see. I asked: "See whom?" I was afraid of hearing this answer: "Your father." She did not answer.

That second day, third night of our love, I let my hand wander over her and she responded to its gentle pressure, Virginie offering me her face, her breasts, her belly, she turned away, turned back and for a long time, angry with my hand for not being made of clay, I stroked in turn Virginie's face, breasts and belly, my hand grew tired, I was going to exchange it for the other, she took advan-

145

tage of the respite to ask: "Your book?" I let my hands drop. Since our love I had thought of the book in flashes now and then, embarrassed, remorseful and without even trying to find out how to defend myself against it, I had found the solution, it was to press myself against Virginie. I squeezed her hard enough to stifle her, I stifled the book. It died in our groans. Once, however, getting my breath back beneath Virginie lying across me, heavy, inert, I saw myself as Joseph Smith in my prison at Carthage, Illinois, the mob was lynching me and I wept for those words some of which I had chosen, weighed in the patient scales of my reflection, to see if they were capable of enduring this journey and worthy of it: two hundred and fifty pages to the end of the book, one thousand five hundred miles to the Promised Land, the other words I had received in surprise, in wonder and kept for their foreign ways, how could I distrust them when they had come so far, from those provinces where I, Joseph Smith of Vermont, had never set foot: the Carolinas, California, Canada, I wept for my people of words already far behind me their leader, who was dead, who was becoming another and I saw my work interrupted at less than halfway, one hundred and seventy pages, one thousand five hundred miles still to be covered, I knew that another would come and take my place, my succession, I saw him: Brigham Young, by way of Missouri, Nebraska, Kansas, Wyoming, Colorado, bringing to a successful conclusion and to the last words: the end, *The Journey to Virginia* in which he had changed one word of the title: *The Journey to Utah.* I said to Virginie: "Let us make love again. I don't love my book any more."

She let me slide her beneath me and I took her without her giving herself, her body went with my body but her face had frozen and her arms were beating a different rhythm, on either side. I guessed that Virginie was in a state of equilibrium, incapable of choosing between submission and refusal, tenderness and anger and I possessed only half of her, the book had cut her into two parts, one for it one for me, then Virginie's hands fell on my back like stinging slaps, their nails scored me and I thought: this is your punishment—I accepted it gritting my teeth and accompanied my painful pleasure with pictures in which my sister and I, children at the seaside, were frantically tearing up the pages of the book which waves were fighting for at our feet and their tongues were licking my toes, then I saw them as packs of bitches which had come from far away, come from me, at the last page they lapped my belly and on Virginie's moist lips, on which I was sucking salt, I saw the question forming again: "Your book?"

I drew away from her to return to my place, beside her, I would have liked to make my slow movements even slower, my arms, my fists scarcely made any impression on the bed and I remembered that in those books which she sometimes read five or six in a row, a thousand or twelve hundred pages in an afternoon, hundreds of thousands of words which Virginie received all at once, all of a piece, she used to emerge dazed, red-eyed and I looked through four of those books to find out—I remembered that they all tell stories of men who are struck on the nape of the neck to send them to sleep—the instrument: the butt of a revolver, a bludgeon, a wrench, a bottle—and the author always remarks that the victims smile. I know why. It is because each victim has fallen into his kingdom, his landscapes, he is walking with his sister at the seaside and holding her hand, she is his unquestioning mistress, who understands everything, asks for nothing and both of them, with sand and water stretching away into the distance, have sand and water thoughts in which time is drowned, buried so that they never feel the need to swear eternal love for one another and I said to Virginie: "Let me sleep," but she said:

"The book? Why this sudden repugnance? Tell me, I have nearly stopped feeling angry."

"Because of you."

"Idiot! One day you will love me less or not at all. . . ."

"No."

"And I for my part shall love you, perhaps not not at all, but less, much less. . . ."

"No."

"And I shall be somewhere else with others, somewhere else for others telling myself, without believing myself, that it is for always, just as I tell myself that today with you and without believing myself . . ."

"No, Virginie, no."

"Turning around, I shall see you farther and farther away, you will be shrinking, let me finish, then one day turning around as usual, it will happen like this, I can see it already: I open my eyes, I see nobody, I think I have made a mistake, I shut them, I make a silence within me, around me where a lover is moving about, still nobody, I think I have made a mistake, I make a noise and he does too, I open my eyes, still nobody, then I start to blackmail my feelings, I drum up my happy memories, my sad memories, all in vain—and I understand that I shall not find you and shall never find you again."

"You will find me, Virginie, you will find me. . . ."

"Never again and you too, for your part, you will make a noise, a silence and you will blink your eyes. You will try to remember, without success, whether I was a blonde. For you I shall be an insignificant total of gestures, a voice without any timbre. Oh, I know that our extinction will take time— and to all appearances you will be motionless waiting for me, but there will always be something drawing us apart, do you know what?"

"I think I know, Virginie, it's . . ."

"Idiot, you were going to say time, you must say: life."

"No, no, not life, death . . ."

"Exactly, exactly . . ."

Virginie needed to walk about, perhaps to run about. She paced around the room. For a long time I watched her, tense, naked. Then I lowered my eyelids. Her body intensified the darkness when she passed the window; if she moved away, the light from the streetlamp struck me: a light so cruel that I turned my head away, wondering whether Virginie, without my hearing her, had opened the curtains. I wanted to be somewhere else, I could not get there. It seemed to me that my sister had taken me out of myself and I could see the carriages, the landscapes, the big animals far away in Virginia

about 1842, they were looking for me, I was waving to them, we could not manage to get together.
I ran toward them while they glided toward me
and when I thought I was approaching them Virginie reached the maddening point of her round,
the end of the curtains which she had just passed.
The light mowed down my friends. Between two
flashes I recognized the trees in the landscapes,
they were fluttering their leaves, the men and
women in their wagons, they were waving colored
scarves, the eyes of the big animals, they were
shedding my tears.

Virginie wiped them away with the back of her
hand which I saw swooping down on me, which I
tried to push away and which she stopped just
short of my face. It was almost a caress, which
brought me back to her body. This was moving
slowly, and I had put myself on my side so as not
to lose it behind my head over which Virginie
trailed her fingers every time she passed, then, at
one moment, she placed her hands on her body,
smiling she felt herself, massaged herself, molded
herself and I said to myself: Virginie doesn't exist,
Virginie is inventing herself, I would have shouted
with pleasure if I had not been afraid of cutting
short the dance which she was doing twice over, in
the room and on her body where, with her fingers

now closed together and now spread apart, she was covering and uncovering surfaces which I reproached myself for having failed to embrace properly, and Virginie spun around, her head held high, as if she could not see me and yet I think, today, that all through the dance she must have been aware of my feelings: fear, surprise, interest, and finally frenzy, for she stopped just as, unable to contain my love and remorse any longer, I jumped out of the bed and Virginie pushed me away and lay down saying:

"Exactly. Death. One day I shall grow tired of you and I shall leave you, because of death. . . ."

"What do you mean, Virginie?"

"Because of death which you forget, you love me as if I were destined to live forever and you never to disappear. . . ."

"I don't think so, Virginie, I often think about death, you know, it even seems to me . . ."

"No, I can tell from your way of seeing me and taking me that you see me and take me with a sort of calm or certainty, you are sure of seeing me and taking me whenever you like, tonight, tomorrow, and a thousand years from now, tomorrow and a thousand years from now is all the same to you, you behave as if we weren't threatened. . . ."

"No, Virginie . . ."

"And I shall leave you one day, if you don't change. . . ."

"What do you mean, Virginie?"

"Just now, I wanted to make you say: it's life. I stopped you in time, you were going to say something else and I would have lost my temper. But the fact remains that, if I played safe, I wouldn't change a word of what I said: one day I shall be somewhere else with another, then another, somewhere else for others. . . ."

"No, Virginie . . ."

"But living, and on this point I think we can agree, living is also fighting against life, its obstacles, its facilities, living is taking life against the current, going upstream instead of down and if you like, if you can, I am willing to abandon myself to the feeling that our love will last as long as we do, and not only abandon myself, but be on my guard so that my longings and desires shall be longings and desires for you. . . ."

"Yes, Virginie . . ."

"A great love, how can I put it, an eternal love, but you will have to change. Do you like it?"

She had gotten up, Virginie, she had put on her nightdress and was lying down again. I was going to ask her what she was thinking of when she said: "Do you like it?" She took my hand which she passed over her body, like her own hands a little earlier when she was dancing, spinning and Virginie paused at the bumps, the hollows, the smooth surfaces, she kept repeating: "Do you like it?" and once it was "Do you like them?" I answered: yes—and I squeezed them, then:

"And do you like anything else?"

"Yes, Virginie, I like you the way you are inside. . . ."

"And you aren't afraid of losing me?"

"No, no, I don't think about it. . . ."

"How do you see me?"

"I don't see you. I see us."

"For a long time?"

"Where we are, the two of us, I can see sand, water, stretching away forever. . . ."

"Idiot!"

The word came out, hard and sad. It had scarcely touched me, the first time, but she had just been speaking too seriously and fiercely for me not to feel that I was an endearing character whose fate depended less on her than on me and I bridled at the insult, I was going to answer her, I was looking for a hard, sad word on which to nail her, but Virginie said:

"You will have to change, become a man, accustom yourself . . ."

"Resign myself!"

"No, accustom yourself to day and night and love them as they are, one after the other, how can we tell which came first and it hurts me to think that you might go on drawing the curtains all your life. Whatever you do, the sun always rises. . . ."

"I know, Virginie, I know. But once or twice, when I was alone in my room working at my desk, I went from one night to the next, it was the same night."

"No, never the same. And I am like the night, never the same. Changing, aging . . ."

She said that word: aging, and I saw them, my father, Indiana, him bent and the mare almost toothless, they had toiled along the Avignon road the two of them, she trotting and my father talking and perhaps he noticed, when I jumped down to catch the bus, the trees with the wind blowing through them, the men and women in their wagons, the big animals shedding tears over Virginia which died about 1842 and I answered: "No, no," but Virginie went on:

"Aging and day after day a little less alive, a little more dead, dying . . ."

"I don't see that, Virginie, I don't see that. . . ."

"And if you are to keep me, I shall have to feel that you know me to be mortal. . . ."

"I don't see that. . . ."

"For it is death which makes me young and beautiful and with you, who shut your eyes to the fact that I must die, I feel neither young nor beautiful. . . ."

I was going to reply: yet nothing matters to me any more but your youth and beauty, but just as I was shaping these words, the futility of the retort overwhelmed me: why state the facts when the facts are staring me in the face? I realized that words must be used for something else and I held them back on my lips in order to replace them with: I love you as much as I loved the book—a sentence which did not leave my open mouth for I reflected that I was risking a great deal and I also refrained from saying: in my book I often state that you are beautiful and if I mention your age only once, that is because you keep it and don't grow older—a provocative remark, I think, in any case she went on without waiting:

"For death makes things young and beautiful and I know why you pass things like a blind man: there is no day, no night for you, consequently no seasons and I remember some almond trees you didn't see, one day, you went past without being dazzled by their white and red flowers, no seasons in other words no blossoming, no beauty, nothing. . . ."

It was true about the almond trees; I remembered too that, on the very evening of the incident, I had promised myself to recount it in my book: I sat thinking in front of my pages, and wondering what I should say further on, I looked through them as if they were full and already finished with, I read the numbers on them, written up to one hundred and fifty so that they should bear my mark and I should feel that they were vaguely familiar, partly tamed, for their whiteness made me giddy, the sheets of paper reminded me of the worm I had found in a furrow, one afternoon when I was following the farmer, one of those maggots which books talk about to our surprise and uneasiness, according to them they have two heads and two anuses and in my closed hand the worm struggled, pushing with one or the other, how was I to know, and I carried it to the estate to place it on a square patch of cement next to the forge, but the worm, instead of staying there, tried to reach the loose soil at the edge of the cement and it would probably have got there, after a day of trying, if every morning I had not run to pick it up and put it back in the middle of the square where I would have liked it to make its home and I imagine that I said to it: don't go forward, don't move and you will never grow old —Indiana squashed it, she must have been looking somewhere else—I saw the white sheets of paper in front of me move and place themselves one behind the other, each one the ring of a worm, two or three hundred rings, two or three hundred pages which without stirring any further reached a point in space where I could not recapture them either by hand or thought and the worm chanted: run, catch me, catch up with me, run as fast as you can, I shall always be in front . . . , an unbearable litany and I cut it short by telling myself: the only way to get the worm back to the middle of the square is by filling the white pages—I sat thinking, therefore, the very evening of the day it happened, about that incident of the almond trees and I was wondering whereabouts in the book to place it and how to express my indifference to trees and flowers, when I suddenly felt myself blushing and faltering: I would never have the courage to admit to that defect, more than a defect, a taint, what would my readers think, what impression would they form of me—and Virginie, I could see her discovering my taint written in black and white and exclaiming: "Yes, that's it, I noticed it, I told you about it . . . ," in black and white and after that it would be no use my trying hard to see and exclaiming ostentatiously: look at that tree, how splendid it is—for her I would always be the cripple and I told myself that it would be best to conceal the thing from the

readers, from my sister, to deceive them, an abom-
inable course of action, admittedly, and what if the
book was to suffer as a result, limp or stammer at
one point, and if, now that I had begun, I got into
the habit of lying? I saw the book a different book
from mine and myself a different person, I stood up
to go and join Virginie in the next room, when the
idea struck me of recounting, revealing that she
can only see things as they are and that she does
not possess within her the most beautiful trees,
whose roots are in Virginia and whose branches are
in me, trees whose trunks, on evenings when I feel
lonely, lean across the Atlantic and I recognized
myself, reconquered myself, I passed my hands
over my face like caresses, I felt affection and
admiration for myself and I had no doubt that the
passage would be beautiful, in my book when I
wrote it, toward the middle of the second part: yes,
tainted, but I have the gift of seeing trees which
are not right in front of me—an exhilarating
thought so that Virginie did not hurt me when she
reminded me of my past blindness before the almond trees, I felt jubilant and I would willingly
have pitied her, if I had dared, but she went on:

"Perhaps I shall stay with you all the same, if you
change, then there will be more fire in your caresses, more fervor; they will rise convulsively

from the very depths of your being, where you know that I shall be old, one day, and ugly perhaps. . . . Then with me and close to me you won't be somewhere else, detached. . . ."

I was still looking at that idea, those pictures: the trees which are not in Virginia but in me and I was following what she was saying from a distance, she continued:

"Imagine if we were to live forever, we would put off our desires to the next day, for a hundred years, we would think: I have plenty of time, all eternity—and there would be no sense of urgency any more. . . ."

"You think so?"

"Yes, no sense of urgency any more about anything and if I reproached you with making love badly, you would reply: I will do better tomorrow, in a hundred years, be patient—and you would never do anything well, because you would have all eternity in which to do better. . . . You see?"

"A little, Virginie. . . ."

"Look at the women, the men around you, one life is already too long for them. They grow tired. So imagine what it would be like if they had eternity! Can you see us, you and me, spending eternity together?"

"Not very well, Virginie. . . ."

I could see perfectly well and did not dare say so: Virginie and I are a thousand years old and are just the same as today: she at twenty-one, I seventeen, we have not moved, we still have the same blood which I imagine to be red because it is young and I take Virginie then, when we have finished, on the bed on which I sprawl I say to her: before, when time existed, you could reckon that human beings, in the course of their life, repeated ten thousand times what we have just been doing. Ten thousand times, just imagine, you might as well say never. And then I'm being generous in my calculations. But now that a human life cannot be summed up in figures any more, I must admit that if time had not died, I would never have had the desire or the courage to take you after the nine thousand five hundredth time, indeed I think that as early as five thousand I would have marked time and started calculating, I would have become thrifty with my person, sparing of my love, parsimonius with my remaining strength. You would have heard me cry out to you: no, no, no more love, let us put it off— and see, Virginie, how blind you are: you would have left me because I would have been afraid of loving you, in other words of dying and you would have gone with boys who were less thoughtful, impatient to commit suicide—see, Virginie, how blind you are: you would have left me because people die and not on account of eternity.

I imagined us, Virginie and me, in another way too, namely:

Time is not dead and goes on passing, flowing on, but it has eternity before it as we have eternity before us, time passes and there is no youth or old age any more, we do not stay Virginie at twenty-one, I at seventeen, we are respectively ten thousand and twenty-one, ten thousand and seventeen and we count the years for fun, to be happy, on a page so big that we have papered our room with it, we record the time with strokes, one stroke a year, in a thousand centuries we shall change the paper and at the last stroke I take Virginie, indeed I take her *all the time* and I say to her: you see, I have the same strength, the same love today. . . .

"What are you thinking about?"

"Just nonsense, Virginie. . . ."

"It's for all those reasons that you must go on with your book. I know very well that I shall never change you completely, with me you sleep, you may be in Virginia a long time ago and I wonder whether out there, at that time, you aren't with some other girl. . . ."

"No, Virginie, that isn't true, out there I'm with you. . . ."

"So you *are* there?"

"No, not really. . . ."

"If you like, we'll go to Virginia one day, tomorrow even, I've got enough money. . . ."

I felt my mouth go dry, it tasted like rotting flesh, I said no, Virginie, no, I don't want to go there, everything has changed. . . .

"Everything has changed. . . ."

"Exactly, exactly . . ."

"No, Virginie, I'd rather stay here, in our room, we are so happy here, the two of us. . . ."

"Just as you like. But you must go on with your book. And write it the way I told you, as a piece of mockery, in order to grow up. That *is* how you've begun it, isn't it?"

I said yes.

"You promise you'll go on with it?"

I said yes.

"Write it so that time passes and I remain."

She bent over, I loved her so much, Virginie, I loved her eyes so much and much more than her eyes, everything about her: outside, inside, I said yes again.

I set to work once more. I read through all that I had written, right away, eighty pages not counting the words on scraps of paper, and for a moment I felt like tearing it all up to begin all over again, I saw myself constructing short sentences, one, two lines, not more except on evenings when I was carried away, when I would go as far as three lines, a reckless folly which I mastered with those full stops Virginie liked so much and I told myself that with short sentences I might succeed in changing, in accordance with Virginie's wishes and will, in accordance with mine too, and I believe that my sister is right, I feel like her that short sentences carry within them time, death.

I abandoned this idea. I had reached the point in the book where I start taking an interest in her, showing her and it would be best to write in a different style from then on. My father, Indiana, Virginia, the Seminoles would have been unable to stand my speaking about them in short sentences.

I accordingly set to work again. Not without difficulty, at first, especially as I worked early in the day as I used to when I was alone in my room and I had to uncover Virginie, climb over her, then cover her up again, actions which I could not manage to perform quickly and I decided to escape from her with my eyes shut so as not to see her, beautiful, naked, breathing and sometimes sighing for however careful I was not to wake her, she was vaguely aware of my departure and Virginie guessed that I was tempted, after silencing the alarm-clock bell, to stretch out again beside her: one afternoon my mistress came home from a department store with a set of high-necked nightdresses made of a material so coarse and rough that it reminded you of homespun and perhaps shrouds are made of that grim, hopeless fabric. I prefer not to think about that.

They were full nightdresses and Virginie no longer had any breasts. I had to hunt for them, I offered thanks to the nightdresses. It is a game you never weary of and only Virginie had the strength of mind to bring it to an end.

She decided that on the twenty-fifth of August I should give her a passage of the book. We were at the beginning of the second half of July. I could not say for sure whether this gave me enough time. Virginie was honest enough to warn me that she could not guarantee that she would keep her promise to wait until that date and I did her the service of sending for a locksmith who fitted the drawer where I kept my papers with an iron lining and a lock.

Until then I had written without asking myself many questions or suffering real torments. I let myself go and sometimes all the speed of which my hand was capable was inadequate to follow a pen which seemed to me to scratch and scribble by itself, inspired, crazy. Behind it, I made myself inconspicuous and now and then I thought: if only it lasts! It lasted. Every morning I took the pen, wiped away the traces of its outing the day before and we set off on some trial trots and gallops. We tried to recover the impetus which had been broken by sleep. The pen did not wake up easily. When I thought it was ready to go, it would drop off to sleep. Never very deep. I could feel a growing excitement, sense a frenzy. It sprang forward. Long afterward, two or three pages further on, we paused to get our breath back. Between my tired fingers, the pen trembled with my intoxication.

Often I swore to myself that I would abandon it, one day, when it was going at a gallop. Then I would not be behind it any more but beside it, with my hands in my pockets.

A pen, in fact, which loved only long sentences, a pen with plenty of wind and which never forgot its commas, whenever it drew breath or got its breath back. I defy anyone to say that it left any out, even a single one. I held it, it twisted my hand gently when it came to a comma and that was a pause which banished the threat of cramp. My drama is in my pen.

From the moment when, in all good faith, I tried to follow Virginie's advice, the pen between my

166

fingers became a stranger to me. I was thinking too much about full stops and about those disguised full stops that are semicolons not to annoy it. To begin with, surprised, it turned a deaf ear. I, out of love for Virginie, forced it to retrace its sentences. I now know that you cannot tug at a pen's reins with impunity. Mine stopped going forward by itself. At the halts I imposed on it, it behaved as if I had decided to keep it there for hours. It refused to set off again. I spoke to it in a whisper, then in a loud voice, I remembered the shouts used by my plowman friends, I flattered, cursed, threatened. All in vain. Once I changed pens. With no success. Then I took it back: after all, it had written the eighty pages of my book. I turned my sadness and rancor against myself, I said to myself: you are a failure, a good-for-nothing then, modifying my opinion: no, that isn't true, you are exaggerating but this task is beyond you, you don't realize, perhaps it isn't given to you to write a book. I saw my father, Virginie, they asked me: "Well?" And I answered: "I haven't been able to finish my book." I took pity on myself in order to soften the pen's hard heart. Sometimes it set off again but the halts were all the longer in that it had agreed not to wait an eternity. An eternity! I was discovering an eternity in which I would have stayed without writing a single line, a single word. I hated eternity, I was all in a fog. My head formented forests of whips and I struck the pen, I struck myself.

Virginie tempted me most of all when I was undergoing these tortures. Not that I would have neglected her in victory. But what victories had I? Long sentences, defeats. I found them long when I read them over. To avoid deceiving Virginie, to be able to take her without much remorse, I would venture a couple of full stops. Then I would remove one, unable to tolerate it. Remorse weighed more heavily upon me, yet without paralyzing desire. I became cunning: for example, I never ventured to put three, four full stops. I would have suppressed two, three. With two and three, the remorse would have been too keen. I would have been ashamed of caressing Virginie. I would have been taking advantage of her.

Thus I won a few near-victories. With Virginie I was in the book, I took her while thinking of it and full of it. I cried: I love you—I loved the book. Virginie could feel that a third party was sharing in our pleasures. She asked me once: is it the book? I nodded. She did not experience any jealousy and, on another occasion, Virginie told me: it will go when the book is finished. She even showed a certain complaisance, deriving pleasure from this idea or picture: that the book was taking her, the book and not I. A coupling which struck us, I cannot say why, as curiously sweet.

But dismal days and nights went by in which four sentences preoccupied me for two hours to no purpose, for I crossed them out at the beginning of the third. I fought against a longing to sleep, to make love. I thought: I want to explode, I want to scatter myself. I loved Virginie with a love which would not have brooked delay, hesitations, the realities or pretenses of modesty. With a love which would have thought it mad to put off love-making till later, on the pretext that there are certain times for it—and therefore other, unsuitable times. Virginie was always ready.

Soon, however, my bursts of passion began to worry her. For example, one day I had been at my table for a long time and she at hers or lying down reading, dreaming, sewing, examining in a mirror the wrinkle at the corner of her left eyelid, in that late afternoon our last words had been at lunchtime, twice already since the morning I had flung myself upon her and since the morning I had been composing, decomposing, recomposing the same sentence—I rushed at her: I enveloped her, covered her. I twisted her arms, which were as long as sentences. Virginie cried out, asked me: "Do you need me?" I answered yes. It was true.

But once love had been consummated, I had to go back to the table, to the chair, to the pen, go back to the book. I took the longest routes: those which lead to the handbasin where you wash, comb your hair, shave, those which pass the shelves where you take a book to look for an essential detail which may give you the necessary impetus, start everything going again, those which end up at the window where you lean on the sill, lingering there to have a breather and, as the saying goes, to freshen up your ideas. I came across the bed where, with Virginie lying down again, I needed, wanted her again. My mistress guessed my dilemma.

But then she could not decide whether she should give herself or refuse herself. On certain days she put on the perforated, lace-trimmed, fringed nightdresses; at other times, and soon more and more often, she covered herself with the others, the coarse ones. The book was still there behind them. I did not count on finding it there but there I hoped to forget it. Virginie tried to find out when to reward me or punish me. And in what way. However young and ardent I was, she could not believe that my bursts of passion were due to my blood, to my love for her and to that impression of isolation which, I explained to her, comes from the book and can drive a man mad. I hurled myself onto her and already my lips, my hands were roving and she asked: how many pages? I: none. She: how many lines? I: none. She: how many words: I: four, which I shall keep. She said no, Virginie pushed me away, she sent me back to the book.

At other times it was yes, in spite of the four words, perhaps because of them. As if she thought that love would bring on the rest. At yet other times it was no, in spite of nearly half a page, as if she thought that I was asking too much and that love would prevent the rest, the complete page. So I lied. I said that I had written a lot. Virginie scented the lie and said: "Show me." I went back to the table and, from a distance, I showed her some pages I had written a long time before. Virginie did not seem convinced. She gave herself grudgingly, lent herself. Or else did not give herself. We were in a state of complete anarchy.

Even the nightdresses had ceased to mean anything. I took Virginie in the stiff ones, I saw her evade me in the transparent ones.

Everything started with the short sentences. I remember the time when my sister had not yet imposed her will on me: on her, under her, beside her, breathing out or drawing breath, I have my pictures. I am their king. They come from America or from the America in my book. Before our lovemaking: wagons pulled by mules, and several riders escorting the convoy; they are slowly making their way toward the West through the tall grass, it is hot and the wheels which are creaking, which have been creaking monotonously for so long that no one hears them any more, are also part of the silence; wagons and riders would fill my retina until the evening, when the leader of the expedition will call a halt and the fires will be lit, if it were not for the fact that Virginie gives a sigh or that a woman, a child perhaps, dreaming under the covers, has groaned. Then three bears take the place of the convoy: they are looking for honey. The day I lose my memory, I shall have enough left to remember that Davey Crockett, who killed several hundred with his musket or by felling them to the ground, called them *vermin*. Crockett is dead, I smile and the bears nuzzle the beehive; a swarm in the sunshine and either Virginie has given another sigh or I was afraid of the maddened bees, for a herd of bison fills my retina at present, and I see them and also, thanks to them, I see what, sixty yards apart, John Smith recounts in: *True Relations of Virginia,*

Richmond, 1608 and William Byrd in: *The History of the Dividing Line and Other Tracts, from the papers of William Byrd,* Richmond, 1866: that the Indians cover themselves with white wolfskins, crawl up to the herd and kill, with their arrows, one, two, sometimes three bison out of about eighty, stupid animals according to the naturalists but I say: ingenuous animals, trusting animals. Virginie has groaned so loudly that the Indians on my retina stop their slaughter, in any case they would not have gone on shooting: they have enough fresh meat for a day and dried meat for several weeks, I say: meat, and I think: flesh, for Virginie with a squeeze of her fingers lets me know that I must not wait so much as one second, one vision longer and on her, while I lie panting, the pictures whirl around. Within me there is a wind alternately violent and tense which scatters them, sucks them in, drives them away again only to take them back, ebb and flow. On Virginie's shoulders I stroke the wheels of the wagons, the runaway mules, the fur of the guzzling bears, I stroke the bumps of the bison and bears. I listen to an earth-quake which quiets down, subsides. I have rolled to one side of my mistress and all the pictures have come back onto my retina, slow, tired, they are going at a walking pace. Night has fallen on the wagons, the bears have finished the honey, the bison have cropped the grass and the Indians are eating their victims' tongues after putting away the white wolfskins. If I were not afraid that Virginie, in response to my question and perhaps without having answered it, would ask me where I was, I for my part, during our lovemaking, I would ask her: Where are you usually, and just now where were you? I come back to our things, our clothes, our habits: our world. I have to shout to make Virginie hear under the shower: let us make love again.

We did. I say: we, although I was not the same any more. Virginie had satisfied me and, once that had happened, the idea would never have occurred to me, more than an idea: the urge to think of a superior Virginie living somewhere in the world, perhaps a few steps from my room. My submission to the short sentences created that other Virginie: hard, virile. I credited her with furious thoughts, sadistic appetites, cruel instincts and I imagined her with enormous fingernails, for heaven knows what pleasures and what torments. I wanted to suffer. Sometimes I said—and Virginie all but heard: bite, scratch, strike wildly, mercilessly. She was puzzled by these mumbled words and urged me to speak clearly. I told her some lie for I was afraid that she would take fright and consider me abnormal. Then she would have rolled her eyes, she would have run into a corner of the room and there, like an animal, she would have been afraid. I imagined Virginie like that, just as I was speaking to her. We would have become strangers to one another. And, seeing from her face that she no longer recognized me, I would have lost my head.

I kept it, in spite of the new pictures. I would never have believed that they had impressed me so much, those illustrations you see, as a child, in history books: Louis XI and the cages, the wheels. Virginie opens the door of the cage. The sunlight plays on her fingernails. Then I see the wheel. Some executioners drag me along, stretch me out on the spokes, pull on the ropes around my arms, my ankles and, satisfied that the knots cannot come undone, tighten some screws, and also some vices or so it seems: those drawings in the history books are not very clear. But I remember the horses very well: Virginie is in charge of them. She picks up the loose end of the ropes and ties some more knots on the horses' collars. She hits them to make them move. My bones crack. Virginie stops the horses by stroking them. Then hits them again and again my bones crack. Just as they are on the point of coming apart, Virginie, trembling violently, alternates blows and caresses. The horses halt, move off again, I gently lose my limbs and the more I die the more Virginie restrains the horses. My death agony is drawn out. I love, hate these pictures.

Once, in the middle of the night, I was halfway between wakefulness and sleep, looking at Virginie and her fingernails: she spoke to me but that voice, which I found attractive, was not hers. Suddenly I understood: it was a man's voice. I sat up, my forehead, my hands damp with sweat, Virginie was asleep beside me. My heart was pounding wildly, a stranger, it was beating for itself, too full of its own terror to match mine. I thought to myself: the taste for men! I lived through that passage in my book where I tell how, in connection with the almond trees, I passed my hands over my body and my face to recognize myself, become aware of myself, make sure that I was myself. I shut my eyes, which were prickling with sweat. Lying down again, I pressed myself against Virginie and told myself: if you feel that men are beginning to attract you, if Virginie, male and warlike, obsesses you much longer, you must confess to her that you are changing and that vice is threatening you. I had no doubt that she would urge me to abandon the book, to throw its pages into the fire so as to see them no more, think no more about them. Or else Virginie still thought that I must go on with the book to the end. And she would add: in long sentences.

Tempted as I was, I did not wake her for all that. Her voice would have reassured me. But we would have taken our pleasure and I know myself well enough to know that, if it had been imperfect, I would have considered it ambiguous and from that failure I would have deduced reasons for believing that I was alone and destined for misfortune.

Toward the end of the morning, we used to set off for a beach which, apart from a few fishermen, was frequented only by the birds, which left marks. To get there, we had to walk along the sands for an hour, climbing over dunes or going around them. There I discovered that I had lost my pictures of America and I thought, at that time, forever. Under a sun so hot that she no longer had the strength to speak, my sister stretched herself out. I did the same, a little way from her. We would have stayed there for hours like corpses if the rays of the sun had not been so scorching. Virginie turned over, moved the towels about on her. Stood up, swaying slightly, and walked down to the water. She swam about. Then she came back and lay down again, silent. Without any memories perhaps. A towel over my face, I lay motionless in a sort of hole, or rather box, which I had scarcely needed to hollow out. I felt a certain moistness. A box, a coffin.

With my eyes shut—the sun irritated them so much that I had to shield them with my hands—I turned my face toward the sky. Its rays were flashes, patches, broad surfaces, masses, successions of dots and complex figures, like those I have seen in anatomical plates in which cells are enlarged by the microscope. I waited, dozing gently, for the pictures. Virginie brought me back to reality with her fingernails, the cage, the wheel. Then I tried to limit the visions and, to bring them into existence, I invented the wagons, the big animals, the trees. These pictures did not last for long and broke up or remained in a haze. I could not recognize anything any more. The pictures of the will are not to be compared with those of the dream, of the drifting brain. The former have neither the solidity nor the beauty of the others. When I thought I was holding one, of those which, without my thinking of them, without my dreaming of them, came so easily to me in the past, I found that the sun had pierced the towel and my cheeks were burning. I shifted about. That is enough to vex a vision and put it to flight. My father says so, in my childhood, at the beginning of my book: "I can never warn you sufficiently against the things which can be seen, which can be heard, which can be touched. . . ." I looked at, listened to, touched my body. I hate it.

I copied Virginie: she was sleeping, I slept. In the sea I went on sleeping. The sun went down, we set off on our way home and a voice said, inside me: one day less, I could have done without the voice.

One evening, we were coming back from the beach and Virginie, scarcely affected by the sun which had been beating down on her for hours, was talking, walking with wonderful vivacity. From behind, I was admiring her legs and her delicate ankles. I cut off Virginie's feet and I equipped her with bird's feet: she left the same marks in the sand as they do, light and clear. I thought: tiredness lifts Virginie up, it weighs me down. We reached the staircase leading to our room and I went up first, my imagination obsessed by Virginie's bird's feet. I opened the door and, on the threshold, I stopped. My sister was just behind me, she bumped into me. I could feel that the blood had drained away from my face, I was breathing in little gasps, open-mouthed, I should have liked to be cold and, when I turned around to read Virginie's eyes, I saw them searching, small, anxious, over my shoulder. I said: "I think . . ." Then we went in. Something had altered in the room. We realized that. Slowly, Virginie on the right, I on the left, we ventured a few steps, our eyes riveted to the floor as if we were going to find there, and not in the air, what? A sign, a trace, the marks left by the toe or the heel of a shoe, a scrap of paper, some ash, anything and on my brain which was as rigid as a screen these pictures followed swiftly one after another, pictures of everything, pictures of nothing, words. I thought too of a smell. We searched in vain. I took the key, I walked unsteadily toward my old room, I had a feeling that somebody had, if not tried to force the door, at least pressed against it to open it. Sure enough, the latch was on the edge of the hook. Without going any farther, I went back into Virginie's room. And there I saw it, the book, it had been placed on the table and opened: that big book on the Canadian Indians, so big that we had not noticed it. Blinded. My father had moved the volume from the shelves to the table in order to mark his visit. In order to say to us—above all, in order to say to me—that he was alive, that he could see. That he understood. That he was suffering. That he was going to go on suffering, for a long time.

I was inside him immediately, I was he right away. I thought with his mind: my two children, a daughter, a son, don't write to me. With my daughter, it's of no importance. But him? No more letters, no more packages. Why? I'm going to harness Indiana.

He harnesses her. And sets off.

Then I see with his eyes. I am he, I am myself. I leave Indiana near the lamppost. No need to tie the mare. I go upstairs, I turn the handle of the door of the room where I was, where I ought to be. Locked. My father is somewhat surprised, or is not surprised for I know, myself, that I am living with Virginie. We come to her room. We open the door. We see the clothes: my son's clothes, my daughter's clothes, Virginie's clothes, mine, lying about in disorder, mixed up together. A phrase which sends a shiver down the spine and compels reflection: *mixed up together.* There is also, my father smells it and I smell it through him, a certain smell. The bed is not made. My son always made his bed. I always made my bed, before. Through my father I inspect the room, I know, but he doesn't, not yet, he wants proof. He shakes, pensively, the head which I hang in despair. Then we go out, we cross over to my door, my father bends down and there I let him bend down alone, I come out of him. Through the keyhole he sees: the room empty, the walls bare of shelves, the bed without sheets, with just the wooden frame and the mattress. The mattress is rolled up since nobody sleeps in the bed. The bedstead is covered in dust. My father is too upset, I go back into him. And we smell: a stale, fusty smell. My son no longer opens the windows of this room where he never goes any more. I no longer open the windows of this room where I never go any more. We go slowly downstairs, my father and I. We are in pain; we are very old; our grief is so bitter that we have been suffering for a thousand years. That we are suffering no more. Indiana turns her head. I leave my father, who gets into the buggy. He picks up the reins, I should like to seize them and hold them, drive the buggy for him. Indiana sets off. My father has set off. I am alone.

At one point he had taken that book on the Canadian Indians, he had opened it and placed it on the table.

On the mantelpiece Virginie would find a sheet of paper, one of those I used for writing my book. My father told my sister that she would receive, on the first of every month, a postal order in her name, money for her and for me.

I lay down. As on the beach a little earlier and

as on the previous day, I tried to sleep. Virginie went into her bath and, naked in front of the mirror, brushed her hair for a long time. We did not say anything. I listened, I listened to myself. Virginie too perhaps, while brushing her hair, was straining her ears to hear something, to hear herself. I should like her to have heard, as I did, those murmurs made by villages in the morning, in the evening and that other murmur which, together with memories of childhood, voices make within us when we know that we shall never hear them again, voices of the dead. And perhaps, right at the very end, just before she spoke, she caught this noise: something like a door slamming, a rope breaking, a box being shut. She said: "It's finished, don't think about it any more." She had said those words once, I remember and also that I thought of recording them, in my book, at the same time describing the gestures which accompanied them. Virginie stopped brushing her hair, came over to me. Her hand caresses me; I want to say to her: no, nothing is finished, you are wrong, everything is beginning and everything has to be considered, imagined, revised. She said: "Nothing had mattered any more, for a long time, except your book and ourselves." We had forgotten to have dinner. Lying in bed, we did not move, did not breathe. I turned over, my face to the wall. Then Virginie's hand ran over my hair, my shoulders. When I fell asleep, it was still running.

It was hot the next day and we set off for the beach again. I felt a great hole behind me and within me, in the direction of youth. Perhaps it was about that hole that Virginie was thinking, when she spoke of the man I had to be. I should have liked to fill it with words, they did not cross my lips. I could not manage to construct sentences. Virginie was talking enough for two and not once did she scold me for my absentmindedness and monosyllables. Now and then I sensed that she was gauging and judging me with a glance. I knew that that very evening, and even before, on the water and on the sand where there is nobody but the birds, I knew that with her arms, her lips, she would do her best to banish my distress and the memory of things past. You might imagine that gestures and attitudes on the one hand, words on the other, amount to the same thing. No, gestures and attitudes are barren of pictures.

We walked along and I saw her, without looking at her. With her brown skin, Virginie had never looked more beautiful. She asked me to go into the water with her. I refused, she went off, submissive, patient, how could I tell? Then, cool and fresh, she lay down against me. She had plenty of things to relate, stories, even events: the water was lovely; the sun was shining right down to the sea-bed; a couple of fishes had swum between her legs and she would have liked her legs to be those fishes; a crab had nearly pinched her; some sailors had waved to her from a boat out at sea. I listened to her, thinking that life is nothing else: a story of sunshine and water, with crabs, men waving their arms, a happy woman—and time passing at breakneck speed.

We set off. My father's visit dated back to the previous day. Virginie walked around and around the room. I took her and in my head there were a great many men, women, all over the world they were standing on their doorsteps and I saw them again, in a succession of flashes, in their beds, out-side their beds, in the street, the fields, wherever people live, they were saying: yes, it's a great pity, what are we going to do? Virginie clasped me to her, they went on: You've got to live. Words, phrases which never cease to fascinate me, to repel me.

And in order to live, I too, like them, like every-body, I opened the book after an interval of a day and a half. I turned over the pages, they turned them over for me.

I continued without too much difficulty and without looking closely at what I was doing. The pen ran along. Virginie asked: "You aren't forgetting to write properly?" I was flung backward, to the period preceding the visit. Then Virginie went on: "You're writing about the fairs?" And again: "The gypsies, the knife grinders?" I made an effort and remembered. Then: "Yes, yes, a few." I did not know. I could not remember whether I had already described the fairs. Virginie concluded: "It isn't a question of putting one in, to please me, you must put in as many as you can. Your book will be a book of fairs and festivals."

Little by little, I recovered my previous enthusiasm. I wrote fast, I went straight from one page to the next, and every four sheets I put my pen down to read what I had written, I crossed out, cut, added. From time to time I remembered the short sentences and the full stops. I constructed some, I inserted some. Nothing could be easier, really: you write some long sentences and you stick some full stops into them, right through the heart. You murder them. I was revolted by the idea of Virginie reading my book and killing my sentences with her pen. I asked her to make our outings to the beach less frequent. One day in three, or else she should go by herself. My sister did not want to leave me. So it was one day on the beach in three. She wanted to know my reason: "Is it because of the book?" It was because of the book.

She no longer repulsed me, we had no more problems. Virginie sometimes put on the coarse nightdresses. For fun. More often than not, the perforated ones, and my mistress looked solemn, hesitated. Again for fun. I smiled. In my dreams, eagles circled around.

One night, the estate went up in flames. I woke up with a start. Virginie was asleep, calm and, I think, dreamless. Some men were emptying buckets of water, other were playing jets on the blaze, My father was going from one to the other, giving orders and encouragement, and throwing water on the flames too. Then he told them: "I started it." They shrugged their shoulders and looked at the fire, without appearing to have heard. I think my father did not know whether he had done the right thing. Nor whether he wanted the fire put out or allowed to burn to its natural end. The eagles passed to and fro, high up above the flames, and, of course, since the estate went up in flames during the night, I had to be asleep to see it and a prey to dreams. Then Virginie appeared, she too seized hold of a bucket, on the wet white metal I saw her red fingernails.

I had unforeseeable accesses of curiosity and sentences burst from my lips, to my surprise and Virginie's. My questions, incidentally, made her happy. Once I asked her with whom she had lost her virginity and how. Whether she was sorry that it had been with someone other than me. I remembered this remark of Virginie's, something like this, I quote from memory: I should like to see you swamped with women and debts. My heart beat wildly when I imagined Virginie swamped with men. Virginie: "I shan't tell you, I shan't ever tell you anything about that." And I: "Why not?" Virginie: "Because." A poor, stupid answer, of course. But it made my blood tingle. My heart was pounding. Then I described how, in my opinion, the thing had happened. Virginie smiled and did not correct my account. I described the man's gestures, words, I saw a hundred men around her, caressing her. And she, you, Virginie, incurious, resigned, dead beneath the man's weight, and tears on her lashes. On my features and in my voice, there was grief. . . . But no. I am inventing. I know perfectly well that I felt no distress. None whatever. It was Virginie who imagined it. For she pounced on me, squeezed my head, then my shoulders, clinging to them and, with her eyes shut, Virginie said: "You will soon be a man. You are becoming jealous."

I frequently returned to the attack. Frequently I took up again the story of Virginie's deflowering and every time I invented new dialogues, gestures and I pronounced the words they would have had to say, if their embrace had taken place in Virginia about 1842, where all was beauty. In my head, the boy's legs, arms, Virginie's arms, legs were smooth, agile and in the darkness of the bedroom could be seen white flashes, fishes. My mistress listened, pensive and clouds passed over her forehead: memories, regrets, how could I tell? Sometimes I felt that Virginie was disarmed, on the point of capsizing and falling into the pictures. But at that time she was already too old. Indeed she had been for a long time: old, hard, since my father, after their return from the mountains of Lure and Lubéron, had given up trying to save her. I would have had to talk without stopping, I would have had to be time myself. Then I would have ravished, covered my sister. Then we would have been in my country of America, with my father. Too late. Virginie sees only the quaint side of the pictures. She loves only what exists. For example: I was talking to her one morning, and my story was so beautiful, so passionate that Virginie had shut her eyes and was breathing with her breasts. I thought: Virginie will always have her eyes shut, Virginie's breasts will always breathe. She shook herself, she said to me: "When you have told that story a thousand times, at the rate of one story a day, I shall give you the true account. Be patient. Go on becoming jealous."

Of all the words I know—and I know a great many; like a self-educated man, I take dictionaries and read them from cover to cover; but it is not to learn, to know, that I bury myself among the pages of dictionaries: it is to discover the pictures which are inside words—of all those I know, then, the poorest, indeed the only poor one is: jealous. So poor that, I must admit, the word *jealous* fascinates me as much as the richest of words: *areola* for instance. I would beg Virginie: "Tell me what the first time was like," just to hear her reply happily: "You are changing. You are becoming jealous." When she grew tired of my questions and her answer, I lied: I told her that I was indeed becoming jealous, and Virginie said: "Jealous, really?" I would have liked the word to be a thing and I would have opened it, with a knife. A thing! There is in me, there was in my father such a strict sense of logic that, depending on the occasion, I am dazzled and overwhelmed. In my book, I record the explanation my father gave me of eternity in Virginia about 1842. According to him, according to me, words dwelt in things at that time. Every word had its object, its house. Well, I know now that one word set itself apart from the rest, this one: jealous. When the words in that country and at that time, a few years before the Europeans surged onto the continent, rushed into things, each words having its thing and one only, I imagine that *jealous* was asleep, indolent, a sort of dormouse. It awoke too late. The thing which had been destined to receive it (A fruit? A bird? A woman? I?) had dried up. The fruit, say, had died of waiting. That is why *jealous* does not speak, does not evoke any pictures. It is a word which has never become flesh, a word with no nostalgic memories. A word which, if my explanation holds good—it holds good—was not impregnated with Virginia about 1842. An infernal word, I mean a word belonging to hell. It may be that others exist, likewise devoid of pictures. To know for certain, I would have to have read the dictionaries from cover to cover, the big ones rather than the small, and not only read them: I would also have to know all the pictures which are in the words. Then I might discover that there were a great many of them, in Virginia about 1842, which were left behind, forgotten in sleep and darkness. Yes, the theory is sound. One day, if everything worked out, if everything began again, I would offer it to my father as it stands. I can see him from here, I can see his emotion. . . .

My knowledge being so limited, *jealousy*, for

me, is alone of its kind. I hate it, but I could not possibly confuse it with coarse words, which I also hate, as did my father. Yet I did not behave toward coarse words as I suppose that he did. I have Virginie to thank for the discovery that dirty, ugly words are clean, beautiful: pure words, in certain circumstances. About the time I resumed work on the book, after my father's visit, she confided in me that she would like to hear me use foul language, in the midst of our pleasure. I remember her low, hesitant, rather ashamed voice and the violence of my reaction, then my distress. I asked: Why? Why? I found myself in between two pictures: I was sliding down a well, I was sinking out at sea. Virginie started. First of all the coarse words which are not really. Then the real, violent ones and I preferred not to know from what inner region, from what cesspool she was drawing them. Once, without thinking, I copied Virginie, I went so far as to whisper one of those words. It became a habit, and a pleasure. The coarse words flooded me with diagrams in which I could see a foreground which contained us, Virginie and me, and reproduced what we were doing, touching, and the diagrams shrank and lengthened according to a perspective which is unfamiliar to me, and I could see what we were doing, touching in a middle ground which contained the world, the whole of space. At that farthest point, there was always a sky which was swelling and seemed to be falling. The pictures which came from the coarse words when I took Virginie gave me the strange, lasting impression that space and time are one and the same thing. And above all, in the pictures, that sky which was swelling before my eyes.

If, in spite of all that I owe them, I hate coarse words, it is because they are too closely linked with bodies. They exist only by their grace. And when the lovemaking is over, they make hideous corpses. Coarse words are not in the air, outside us in time. Nor are they in our minds. They live with our hands, our lips, everything which rots. I explained this phenomenon to Virginie and I would have liked to tell her that there were no coarse words, in Virginia about 1842.

She thought up games, attitudes, complicated positions, unusual ways of holding each other— sometimes we did not hold each other—and before inviting me to take part in these acts, Virginie always explained them to me. She bent her body, which was naturally supple, to realize these ideas and these pictures from which she expected to obtain added pleasure—and even more: new joys and we would be, according to her, the first humans to experience them. I followed her, as eager as she was, minus her grace and suppleness, and plus something like remorse. We reached the limits of equilibrium, the point at which you fear the two bodies are going to fall and break. I felt that fear up to the moment when, not knowing any more whether Virginie was in front, behind, on me, under me, by my side—it seemed to me that she must have mutilated herself and cut herself into pieces for me to be able to touch, caress, rub her wherever she came in contact with my legs, my hands, my chest—I lost my head. Then, with my eyes still shut, I slowly moved my fingers over her, beginning at her head or her feet and I found, to my delight, that everything was in its place, the face, the breasts, the belly, I would not have been surprised if parts of her had failed to answer the summons. In which case, at the foot, in the depths of the bed where they had rolled, I saw myself looking for them and sticking them together. We came back from a long way away. About this time, she took to painting her body, to surprise and delight me. When she took off her nightdress, my gaze settled on lines, drawings in red and black. She told me that couples, in marriage, outside marriage, sleep after a certain time. I knew this: people who sleep are dead people. I was glad that

Virginie should fight against habits, weaknesses and I thought: against old age, against time which saps desire, by passing. But I would also have liked her to go for ten years without exciting me: I have always known that pleasures wear out the body— and the mind, where the pictures are. I have always known that, even before indulging and overindulging in love. A voice inside me told me that time is not to be fought with excesses, the weapons of the poor. I would feel an urge to run away or, when Virginie was suddenly naked with colored lines, to look somewhere else. I would have had to avoid seeing her. To live with my eyes shut.

After these clinches and clutches, I would lie still. My breath came back little by little. I watched Virginie go over to the washbasin. She ran, jumped, talked. Nothing marked her. Nothing remained on her of the mask which had covered her, while we were taking our pleasure, the mask of love, the mask of death and sometimes, when I brooded over that mask, I remembered my mother on her bed: she had had those slightly hollow cheeks, where you are tempted to place the tip of a finger and to press, to pierce, she had had those cheeks from which the blood has drained away. I told myself that one day and forever Virginie would have the mask. She would wear it and, that time,

I would not be responsible. Yes, one day **Virginie** will display that mask and I will not be the one who has taken her.

She turned off the tap, came up to the bed and, standing over me, very big and very tall, she slapped me with this sentence: "When you die, you will have known everything, experienced everything, what is normal and what isn't, what is as well." Then she assumed a thoughtful look and corrected herself: "Anyway, nearly everything, you will have known, experienced nearly everything." I forgot the slaps, only "nearly" made me think: What remains for you to know, what remains for you to experience? I guessed that Virginie would not stop at the point we had reached, and that the further we went, the two of us in time, the narrower that "nearly" would become and the more I would know, experience those thoughts, those repulsive acts which attract you so that you cannot tell, in the end, whether you should commit them, whether they are good or evil.

Once, I discovered this daydream in me and it has never left me since, full of exhilarating words from which landscapes sprang: I awake, Virginie is not beside me. I wait for her. She does not appear, will never appear. My passion for Virginie becomes (once more?) a passion for words. I am in love with them. I fall asleep with them.

One night, I really thought that my daydream had changed the world. Virginie, who had gone out as dusk was falling, was late returning. At dawn she came into the room. I had almost grown accustomed to her absence. I could feel a question inside me, but so weak, so sickly that it was not born, that I did not ask it. Virginie killed it a second time: "Don't ask any questions!" After that night, she went out once a week. The whole night. The following days, Virginie would buy a lot: things for our room, books, fruit, nightdresses for our nights.

About that time, we were in the middle of August, she took it into her head to help me more actively with writing the book. She stopped saying: "How is it going?", stopped worrying whether I was putting in the fairs, the gypsies, the sheep of childhood. Virginie, every other evening, called me to her, laid me out on the bed, then . . . My passivity, which I mention at the beginning of my book, in a few lines, using these words: *discipline, a predisposition to the condition of disciple,* my passivity went so far that I obeyed her, although I understood why Virginie wanted me beside her and dreaded the story she was going to make me relate. Virginie said: "Tell me what it was like in Virginia, where for such a long time you thought you were living." I replied: "No, no" and tried to get up. Then my sister put on a stern expression and over her face there passed shadows which were not sadness, but something which never fails to touch me: gravity. "Tell me." I said: "No, no, no . . .," many more noes than the first time, but feebler and I could feel that I was going to talk. "Tell me." Then I conjured them up: the trees, the wagons, the big animals, the pioneers, the small amount of civilization that we need and my friends: Lewis, Clark, Joseph Smith, of Vermont, Jefferson, of Virginia, Andrew Burnaby, the author of *Incidents of Travel*, published in 1798, then the rivers with the Indian canoes, around the estates. I began cautiously, with a sort of reserve, waiting for the pictures to arrive and, when I felt them jostling about in my mind, crowding into my mouth, I set off at full speed, giving the pictures their head, I said what it was like in Virginia about 1842 and you see, Virginie, at that time day merged into night so that a single word described a single thing: day, that is to say night, that is to say day— you see, Virginie, how hard it is for me to speak now that we have lost that language! I said how, according to me, and the chroniclers nearly wrote the same in their books where you have to learn to read between the lines, how according to the chroniclers and according to me there were no opposites any more, in Virginia about 1842, for example life on the one hand, death on the other, and again: dream on the one hand, reality on the other and in order to name life death, dream reality the natives, there again, used a single word—I broke off on purpose to find other proofs with which to dazzle, convince Virginie and carry her off to that land whose name she bears, but my sister, impatient, said: "Go on." I talked about the Burnt-Woods, and told how, because of a few drops of blood too many, Indian drops, those half-breeds of Indian women and white men had lost Virginie, more concerned with hunting the bison as in the past than with creating estates, a task which would have distracted them from their hunting and I told Virginie that, because of a few drops of blood, Indian drops, the balance between the state of nature and the state of civilization had been disturbed or, rather, had not been achieved, a future balance and the Burnt-Woods were very close to it, a few drops of blood away, if I may put it that way, Virginie my love, if I may put it that way and she said: "Don't apologize, go on, go on . . ." and I spoke of the bison: thirty million of them in 1750, a disputed figure and according to other experts the herds on the prairies numbered sixty million and according to yet other experts one hundred and twenty million would be nearer the mark, which is amazing but Virginie my love, out of prudence and so that you don't think that I am exaggerating, that I am getting carried away, we shall take the first of those figures: thirty million—and do you know how many were left, a hundred and fifty years later, in 1890? Five hundred. Because of a few drops of blood too many, Indian drops and the natives hunted the animals with white men's muskets . . ., I talked, talked, I could not stop talking and did not want to stop, ever, I felt that, like time passing, I could talk all the time, in other words talk time and perhaps, in that case, if I succeeded in that exploit, time would stop passing . . ., Virginie, for the past few moments, for the past ten minutes, for the past century had been caressing with her hand, upward, downward, her hand went up and down, helping me perhaps to relive and recount what Virginia was like in 1842, the hand became emphatic, insistent and I came back to myself, to my mistress, to the room, to things, to everything my father once denounced, I record in my book that he said: "I can never warn you sufficiently against the things which can be seen, which can be heard, which can be touched . . ." and Virginie declared contemptuously, mockingly: "That's all just words . . .," and I replied: "Exactly, Virginie, words . . .,"

I was filled with a new fervor, I was going to go on talking, but she did not let me continue, she added: ". . . Words, nothing but words and when you have said them, when you have wallowed in them, on them, when you have made yourself drunk with words, then you open your eyes, they fall on me who am waiting, waiting for you, a real Virginia, of flesh and blood—and you fuck me."

I took her, I suffered.

Never had she been more gentle, more attentive to me or more beautiful either, than after these scenes which she apologized for having provoked and she said: "Like that, I feel reassured, you won't put them in your book. . . ." But however kind she was, Virginie could not dispel a smell which was spreading around us and which had probably not threatened her. That smell I believe was the smell of death. I think you have no need to be dead to smell it. I recognized it and named it, in my dreams too, with the eagles, the estate going up in flames and, more and more frequently, my mother as I had seen her, then as I had imagined her, after death, with the maggots hanging onto the edge of a hole in the eyelids.

The day after the scenes Virginie would ask anxiously: "Do you love me? Are you happy?" And I: "Yes, yes."—"You are sure? And you say so in the book?" And I: "Yes, I am sure, I say so in the book."

Time had passed, we were on the eve of that day: the 25th of August. She was going to discover, on the 26th, certain passages in my book, my favorites, which I had chosen for her. At that thought, at that picture: Virginie reading in front of me, while I watched her, did not watch her, spied on her, did not spy on her, shivers ran down my spine. I stopped living, stopped dying. I called for pomp, solemnities, festivities and both of us, Virginie and I, in a patrician house in the South, in America, would be dressed in rich robes. I saw us masked. Virginie was making a ceremony of her reading. Servants, watching her from a distance, brought the pages one by one and placed them before her, bowing. She forgot me, I forgot her. And the ceremony was so splendid, so imposing that it added to the book. Virginie liked those pages, she told me so, I can hear her. Or else she did not like them but hid her disappointment. If she had admitted it, the patrician house would have been swept away, the robes would have been torn, the porcelain and the crystal would have been broken, the servants would have vanished. We would have found ourselves back in the room, she leaning on the table reading and I waiting.

Or else Virginie does not know. She cannot make up her mind: good or bad? The book makes a strange impression on her. My sister's eyes are vague. She admits her perplexity. I was rather expecting it and, consoling her with other words, I refrain from saying to her: in order to understand and like it, you would have to be out there, where you have never accompanied me. I feel a certain pity for my sister. Far from Virginia, she cannot be in my book.

She showed remarkable tact. She did not remind me of my promise, the next day. . . . That evening dragged a little. At other times, however, it took the bit between its teeth. Time forgot itself or fulgurated. We exchanged a few words. We went to bed when it was still night. Then it was day.

Virginie spent a long time washing and dressing. I sat waiting for her. She settled down facing me, with the table between us. Virginie had put on a little makeup. The red, the green, the black gave her a face of great sweetness. She had put on a loose blue dress with a high neck. A serious dress. My hand, on the left, was gripping the book about the Canadian Indians which I intended to pore over while she was reading. Then I handed her the sheets of paper and she immersed herself in:

"At bottom, my father's discourses were not, as I

believed in my youthful innocence, simply traps
to hold the magic of a past and present time, no,
they were also agricultural and household words,
dishcloth words and pickax words, which he employed to root out and remove the seeds, I might
say the eggs which the world laid in us and if our
teachers were the greatest danger, the enemy my
father fought openly and explicitly, we also had
cause to fear our schoolmates, the street, chance,
the air which, over the years, had become so foul
and poisonous that my father resorted increasingly
to warnings and, along the edge of the garden, in
the garden itself, flowerbeds, shrubs, a battle which
he ought to have won first in the village council
against the councillors who dreamed of nothing
but causing trouble, of shifting earth and destroying nests to install water everywhere, to build
blocks of apartment houses as in the towns and it
was without my father's knowledge that they ordered that notice saying TOWN CENTER and planted
it at an intersection of alleyways, a pretentious,
blasphemous cross considering that we had three
hundred houses at the time and a thousand inhabitants and in view of that I can understand
my father giving up hope of saving us both, Virginie so reserved and stubborn and me with nothing but my meekness, which was inexplicable and

therefore unreliable, how, how was he to get us to grow up together in Virginia about 1842?

There are hardheaded people who will maintain that it was merely a coincidence, but the fact remains that my father went off with my sister the day she discovered she was a woman. I have the story from her who has often told it to me and we laughed a great deal at the time. But Virginie, taken by surprise and feeling unwell, had said nothing about it. At my father's suggestion, they spent the morning touring the estate, an expedition in which my sister had taken part on several occasions but of which she had not retained a single memory. On the stroke of midday my father had Indiana harnessed to the buggy. After the reading and the meal he got together clothes and provisions, making a careful choice of each, and about two 'oclock when I had to set off for school, alone, he was still filling a rucksack and a couple of game bags. My mother whom I questioned on my return gave me a vague reply; my father spoke to her very little and I cannot remember any conversations between them, except on Monday morning, a few words about the household matters of the week. I think that he considered her old and poisoned by life. They set off in the direction of Cavaillon, from which point, leaving the Durance on

their right, they took to the roads leading up into
the Lubéron mountains. It was early autumn. They
reached Manosque, then, traveling north, the Lure
mountains, Mont Ventoux and Malaucène, which
the buggy entered on the fifteenth day of the journey, the fifteenth and last for my father and Virginie covered the distance between Malaucène and
our house in one stretch, a return journey at breakneck speed according to my sister and she could
not tell me, but I think I can understand what had
gotten into my father then, a feeling of weariness
or resentment perhaps for he used the whip and
Virginie described to me, in her own words and
her own manner, the former commonplace and the
latter so prosaic that in order to discover the reality
of those two weeks I had to imagine, embroider,
work myself up into a fever, a journey which my
father intended as a sort of initiation and starting
from Virginie's dry account I pictured that drive
through the mountains of the Lubéron, Lure and
Ventoux, steep roads and the people in their black
clothes may perhaps have understood the reason
behind that horse and carriage which the cars
found it hard to overtake and Indiana never saw
them, simply heard them, a noise which she must
have taken for an angry gust of wind, and my
father left even the country roads but that, un-

doubtedly, must have been on purpose and Virginie told me that he was garrulous then and unpredictable, dancing with childlike gaiety around the truffle oaks for he would stop the buggy on the slightest pretext and they discovered, or my father rediscovered, old coaching houses which had all the trouble in the world looking like garages so that they left Indiana and the buggy there, and my father, with a stride which seemed livelier every day, and Virginie, aching and exhausted, followed the sheep tracks with the wind, the sun, forests of beeches, green oaks and pines, almond trees, olives and lavender in which my father rolled about, into which Virginie dropped and they met, at rare intervals for the season was drawing to its close, flocks of sheep with eloquent shepherds and my father went into ecstasies at seeing or seeing again the red-roofed villages under the sumacs and he confided in his daughter that it was like Virginia about 1842, the small amount of civilization we need, so that my sister was afraid that my father would never want to return to the plain but then— it was the evening of the fourteenth day and ever since the morning an eagle had been circling above them, high up in the wind—they found themselves face to face with a team of roadmakers, several dozen men with machines and my father asked questions, curious, thoughtful, shaking his head, suddenly far away from them, from Mont Ventoux, then he looked at Virginie and my sister remembered that gaze of his clearly, years later, it had pierced her shell of fatigue but presumably she did not know how to respond to it, a gaze which probed her, searched her, then my father went away, Virginie at his heels, without saying good-bye, without a word of thanks and I imagine that those men looked for a long time at that bowed figure I picture to myself, in any case according to my sister, according to me, from that moment, the moment of turning back, my father was as inscrutable and silent as he had been open and talkative on the outward journey and they collected Indiana and the buggy and all through the night of that fourteenth day then all through the day of the fifteenth, until six o'clock when they passed through the carriage gateway of the estate, they drove without stopping, this time taking the main road, the one which goes down, often steeply, as far as Carpentras and I can imagine the two lamps at the back of the buggy, two stars jolting about in the night and dying with the day at Carpentras, after that the road is flat as far as Avignon, as far as our village and my father never spoke of those two weeks nor did he ever speak again of

Upper Provence, of those mountains of the Lubéron, Lure and Ventoux which after that journey existed only in his memory, in his mind, like the Blue Ridge Mountains, in Virginia about 1842. It was the autumn. A few more days and Virginia went off to the town, as a boarder at the *lycée*."

Virginie raised an impassive head. The reading had not altered her features, I saw that they were the same at the last word. She said: "More." I handed her the fifteen pages or so which recount what my father told me about words and how we spent the nights on the hills and how we returned home. The passage which includes the sentence: "They hoisted me with halters up an otter path." She read. She said: "More." Then I offered her another passage, further on in the book, which records how I see the two of us, Virginie and me, at Montpellier. About thirty pages, which I had gotten ready all the same. She read, then:

"Shit."

I said nothing.

"And the rest?"

"Yes?"

"Does it go on like that, the rest?"

"What do you mean, 'like that'?"

"Father, Virginia, Indians, bison, a lot of childish nonsense."

"If you like . . ."

"How many pages?"

"Two or three hundred already. . . ."

"You poor kid. . . ."

She repeated: "You poor kid," her eyes were looking through me at something and later on I was to think: perhaps Virginie was looking through me for a different book, hundreds of pages without my father, without Virginia, without the Indians, without the bison behind me, then:

"Give me the pages where you talk about the blacks. . . ."

I looked puzzled.

"About the blacks . . ."

"You mean: the black men?"

"Yes, the slaves. . . ."

"There aren't any, Virginie, I haven't put any slaves in my book. . . ."

"You haven't put any!"

She repeated the same exclamation: "He hasn't put any!", I felt her hesitate, unwilling to believe me, her hand was twisting the sheets of paper in front of us, clawing the book and I saw passing through her eyes, after incredulity, anger and despair, then:

"No slaves!"

"No."

"Why not? Why not?"

"I don't know, Virginie, I didn't think about it while I was writing. . . . In the Virginia my father taught me about, in the chronicles between the lines, there aren't any blacks. . . ."

"But there *were!*"

"I know. . . ."

"You don't like them?"

"Yes, Virginie, I like them a lot, like other people, and even rather more than other people, I remember that I cried as a child, and even later, only yesterday, I cried when I read what writers say in their books, namely that the blacks were ill-treated. . . . Children were parted from their parents, husbands from their wives, they were flogged, they were put in chains and Saint-Jean Crèvecoeur says in his *Letters of an American Farmer*, London, 1782, that he saw a Negro beaten so hard that he died from his injuries. . . . His owners had shut him up in a cage where there wasn't room for an eagle with its wings folded, and the Negro rotted there, in that cage at Charleston, South Carolina. . . . I would like to have been that slave, I was . . ."

"Well?"

"I didn't see any need to put the blacks in my book, they wouldn't have been in their place. . . ."

"No, they wouldn't have been in their place, like the fairs, the sheep, the gypsies, the knife grinders. . . ."

"You do see a little of *them* in the book. . . ."

"Yes, a little."

Virginie laughed, laughed until she cried, then: "No blacks!"

Those two words made lumps in her throat, it seemed to me that she was trying, unsuccessfully, to swallow them while swallowing her weariness, as people say about pride, then:

"How can you talk about Virginia and not mention the blacks, not once?"

"I am well aware that there were a lot of them, that they were unhappy and, if it were necessary, I would die for them, though that would really be rather ridiculous, not doing them any good or me and, if it were necessary, you know, I would tear up my book but I tell you they would have been out of place in it, it is a book in which, so far, nobody dies, in which nobody ever suffers and dies, it is a book with no white or black in it, where the only colors are those of autumn: green, yellow, red, yes, red, a book in which there are not many people, you, our father, me, three whites in all and

212

no more, a book in which there are no people and nothing happens. . . ."

She had stood up and was walking about, around the table, around me and, at one point, she pushed back her hair, which was covering her face, then:

"There aren't any objects either!"

I said nothing.

"I was expecting a lot of precise descriptions and in your book I would have seen, touched, felt a whip, a saddle, a horse, a *palaam*. . . ."

"A what?"

"A *palaam* too, there are nothing but visions. . . ."

(Later on, I was to look in the dictionaries. It is a new word which is not in Littré, but the others says: "*palaam*: sb. (Saddlery). A kind of bit, consisting of two steel bars joined together by a ring."

"Visions conjured out of nothing, mirages . . . Everything I said to you about short sentences has been wasted. . . ."

"Not entirely wasted, Virginie. Perhaps, but for you, my sentences would have been longer, unreadable. . . ."

I was looking at a huge sentence in front of me, without a single stop, with nothing but commas and I remembered what I say about them somewhere: that they are hooks on which time is strangled. Virginie stirred, she was old all of a sudden, drab and ugly, as I once read that people sometimes become, when they have lost a lover, a mistress, a child, and I went on:

"Perhaps if you had not forced me to take short sentences into consideration and to construct a few, here and there in my book, every now and then, perhaps I would not have gotten so far, a few hundred pages already and already I can see the end coming, perhaps once I had allowed myself to follow a long sentence, a solitary sentence, I would be inside it while it moves forward, overflows the paper, the table, no more day, no more night, no more wakefulness and no more sleep and I don't know that I shall never finish the book, that out there, in Virginia, nobody writes, I shall never know that I began a book, once upon a time, a long time ago and somewhere else, never . . ."

Virginie is not listening. I think about my father and what he told me one day, his monologue is in my book, at the beginning, it comes before the passage on the hills: he confided in me, he admitted to me that he had been mad to think that he could find Virginia again, on the estate, by re-creating it as it was, almost as it was and, indeed, passing time is there, I can feel it, I can touch it: it is in "almost," I would close my hand to stifle time if I did not know that it is also around my hand, everywhere—my father said how much he regretted not giving his attention just to words which, in his opinion, would bring back things—but Virginie says:

"I would have preferred you not to write it. . . ."

But I have written it. And I think: I for my part began with words. I am going on with them. To-morrow I shall finish the book, with words. I have written three-quarters of it, perhaps more. I have . . . But I am not yet in Virginia. I am not yet back in Virginia. And I think: is that because of your sister, who prevented you from writing that long sentence? When she gave you the idea of writing, she also gave you the pernicious idea of short sentences. Is it not her fault if you are still where you are in time? And I think: perhaps I ought to burn the book, start another. Perhaps . . . But a long sentence, a book of a long sentence, is it possible? Then I think: what if it is too late? What if even a long sentence, so long that it is unimaginable, invisible—you would have to be in Virginia to imagine it and to see it—what if even that long sentence gave you nothing, did not give you Virginia, gave you just a book? What if Virginia was somewhere else, behind, back in the direction of childhood? I think . . . My head aches and I hear:

"I thought you would become a man. . . ."

"I don't know, Virginie, I don't know. . . ."

"Yes. You will never know anything. You will always be the one who knows nothing and who, in order to know nothing, turns his head away. Death will pick you, or rather you will fall like an overripe fruit, without having prepared yourself to receive the earth. You will have the panic-stricken look of an animal in your eyes, full of tears and in your death agony you will cry: 'No, no,' you will die like a dog, a coward."

She stood up. Virginie picked up her clothes and put them on with slow, deliberate gestures. She was no longer in the room. My head had dropped into my hands. I did not move when she pushed open the door, I had no need to open my eyes to know that hers were flashing and that there was foam on her lips through which her words were passing with difficulty, hoarsely, a sort of barking and I guessed, half-heard: "Stay in the darkness, in slavery, become your father, I have wasted my time and much more than time . . .," I think she also said—this was in between swearwords which hurt—"You don't deserve life . . . ." I thought of that word which concludes a book, a play, the word: irrecoverable. It pricked the tip of my tongue, the tips of my fingers like a thousand twitching ants. I spent a long time wondering, pondering whether I should keep it to myself, or hurl it after Virginie so that it should hit her, mark her.

I brought out the suitcases, three suitcases but, to take away all the books, I needed at least three more. I took some money. Virginie had been away two nights before and her bag was bursting with notes. As I was going downstairs, the absurd idea occurred to me that she might be in the street and that, when I had bought the suitcases, she would come back to our room. I came back upstairs alone. Before opening my door, I looked through the keyhole and I pictured my father again looking at the bare room. I longed to go and obtain his forgiveness. I imagined the scene, I was Lewis and Clark on their return from Oregon, I had arrived at my father's house by river. The luggage took me all afternoon. I looked through the books while I was packing them. I took them off the shelves one by one, in the order in which my father had brought them or sent them. Then I stroked the book, looking through it too. It seemed to me that I was going back toward him, toward my father, page by page. When I went to bed, I took the book with me to read it until I fell asleep.

In the morning I remembered Virginie. She was far away in time and I reflected that perhaps she was also far away in space. I saw myself as Vir-

ginie, I was coming to the room, after my departure, to collect my things. A selfish visit—not a
pilgrimage.

I made three trips, each time with two heavy
suitcases at the ends of my arms, to the square
where the buses are. This was in the morning. I
should be home about noon. I told myself at first
that I would hide in the fields, the vineyards
around our house, until evening. I asked the driver
to stop his bus a good distance from the village.
My descent with the six suitcases aroused a certain
curiosity. The conductor did not ask me any questions but I went so far as to confide in him that
my father was late and that he would arrive soon,
at this place we had agreed on, with the buggy
and our mare. The bus moved off.

I hid the suitcases in the grass and set off, on
foot, across the countryside, avoiding the farm
workers who might have known me or, if they did
not know me, might have recognized me: the may-
or's son, the solicitor's son, who is at school in
town. . . . Then I saw the house and, on the other
side of the street, the estate.

I slipped quietly into the garden, holding with
one hand the bell which would otherwise have
rung as the gate opened. The door of the house was
shut. I pushed it open and, on the threshold, I stood

still, stock-still. My heart was exhausting me. I shut my eyes for a moment. I moved forward along the dark corridor. My shadow disturbed the shadows. I went into all the rooms, those on the ground floor, those on the first floor. Then the lofts, the attics. There I was no longer looking for somebody, my father, I was looking for something, a body. Nobody, nothing and I went out again.

I ran across the street and went on running on the estate, toward the stables. The straw was clean in the place where we usually keep Indiana. I turned toward the light, outside, the steward was waiting.

He did not seem surprised. He must have known that I was on vacation and perhaps he thought that I had spent the month of August somewhere else with my father's permission. The steward, pleased to see me again, asked me if I expected to be staying for long. I didn't know.

"My father?"

"He went off with the buggy two days ago. We haven't been able to find any day laborers this year for the wine harvest. There aren't any left."

"Well?"

"So your father went off in the direction of the mountains, into Lozère and the Causses, with the intention of bringing a few back."

"For us?"

"Yes. The other landowners get men from Spain and Italy."

"Was he planning to stay out there, up there for long?"

"Several days, two weeks perhaps, it all depends on the people he meets, whether they want to come. . . ."

I looked at the sheep pen, the barn, the saddle-room. Then the steward said:

"Ever since he stopped being mayor . . ."

He saw my expression, and asked:

"Didn't you know?"

"No, I was away, I went off without leaving any address. . . ."

"The village council defeated him over that question of the wine harvest. He resigned his office."

I nodded, I understood my father: Spaniards, Italians in dozens, perhaps hundreds for ours is a region of big estates. He dreaded that invasion, the same as over a century ago, in Virginia about 1842. He knows that some of the men, who come with their families, will not go back home and, once the wine harvest is over, will move north and west. Above all, he knows that most of them will settle in the village and the surrounding country. He

thinks: as in Virginia. These men are both immi-
grants and a horde of Indians. In this village here,
our home, away from the main roads, in our village where there is the small amount of civilization
we need, they are going to settle and their humble
folk's dreams, their poor men's dreams will be all
the more ardent in that they know nothing but
poverty. My father sees the implacable metamor-
phosis of the village into a small town, then into a
big town, with that excess of civilization which
makes time pass, men wear away. I understand, I
feel my father so well, the same as before, always
the same that something throbs in my heart, something which is almost joy, almost happiness, I put
a friendly hand on the steward's shoulder and he
says:

"He has changed a lot, your father. An awful lot.
It's all those birds that have upset him, in my opinion. Twice a day he walks around holding a big
sack open in front of him and he picks up the dead
birds. . . ."

"Why?"

"Why does he pick them up?"

"No, no, he picks them up because he loves them.
Why do they die?"

"Because of the planes and above all because
of the fertilizers, the sulphates, the dose is too

strong for them, even the grapes are poisoned. There are birds' bodies everywhere. . . ."

His hand pointed to the sky and I looked at his hand, then at the empty sky. It dropped and I looked at the ground, where the bodies are. I thought about the eagles and, all of a sudden, I saw Virginie again, she did not believe in living eagles, perhaps she would believe in dead eagles, how could I tell, somebody called the steward, he left me.

Nobody has told me what my father did in the Causses, in Lozère. Nobody, because he went off on his own, because he lived on his own, out there. But then nobody had said anything to me about the expedition they undertook, my father and Virginie the day she became a woman, in the mountains of the Lubéron, Lure and Ventoux. On their return, Virginie summed up in a dozen words. At Montpellier she was to find another half-dozen, poorer still, once when I was pestering her with my questions. Virginie did not believe in words, in pictures. For my part, when I learned that my father had set off for the Causses and Lozère, where I have never been, where I shall never go, why should I when I have words, I imagined the reality:

He goes off with snowshoes on his feet, like those he gave me when I was little, so that, in my provinces of Huronia and Iroquoisia, I could walk in the American snow you read about in books. With the buggy he drives as far as Alès, at the gateway to the Cévennes. There, with Indiana too old, the buggy too hard to pull up the steep roads, he leaves them with somebody. Then he walks: across the Causse Noir, the Causse Méjean, the Causse de Sauveterre, which are in the Rocky Mountains, Colorado. Clinging to the cracks in ravines and rock faces are rows of scanty crops, which give the impression of life and my father approaches. He knocks on the doors of tumbledown buildings. Nobody. He goes away, the wind slaps him, he makes his way along paths and tracks which score the gullied hillsides. The sheep tracks are easy under his feet, his step is lighter. He comes across silkworm houses without roofs, without beams, nothing but black walls. Here he dreams. Women used to put the cocoons under their bodices, next to their skin, in order to warm them. A fleeting vision: my father's wife perhaps. As it happens, he is too hot in his rough overcoat. In spite of his snowshoes, he stumbles, my father is no mountaineer. He crosses limestone crags, gullies hollowed out by the wind, cliff ledges, he spurns those villages which are above all words, pictures: La Cavalerie, La Parade, where horses' hoofs no longer raise the echoes of another world. He goes from bare ridges to arid hollows. He is hungry and the eye of our eagles in him has seen an aspen, perhaps an alder, perhaps, who knows, some willows. He finds some houses, one or two. The shutters are closed, held in place, from outside, by a piece of wood. The people have gone. The people? Father thinks: the young ones. He feels immense affection for the old people. He will take some of them back with him.

Here are some old people. Father has knocked on the door, has come in. Both of them, the old man and the old woman, started back when they saw him. She made the sign of the cross, he cried out. Father explains. The old man's hand, holding the cold bowl of a pipe, trembles. His teeth have lost their strength. Father explains gently. They listen, shake their heads and, on the threshold to which they have accompanied my father with infinite slowness, they stretch out their arms and point toward the plains. Father leaves them.

Old people, more old people. Father tells them that they will not have to work for nothing and that he will give them incredible sums of money, such as are found only in fairy tales. They do not see. They are at that point in time where words no longer talk, no longer make pictures. They are people without pictures. Father leaves them.

I calculate two days for the journey to Alès, with Indiana and the buggy. Two days too for the return journey, from Alès where he collected Indiana and the buggy, back home. That leaves six days which my father spent looking for men for whom words are pictures, almost things.

He is an old man on the road. At the moment of the accident—when my father whipped Indiana, or else she bolted, on account of the cars, without the whip touching her, or else my father turned her toward a car and the mare obeyed, who knows —at the moment of the accident perhaps words stopped making pictures. I can see him saying my son, my son, and meeting death, time which no longer passes.

Late every afternoon, after a tour of the whole estate, I come out of the house, where I have changed nothing, I go into the garden, where I have changed nothing, I sit down by the lime tree, which has not changed. There, holding my book, which I read over and over again, I listen to them: my father, Virginie, Virginia, they are inside me, they argue, quarrel, they put forward words, raise pictures and I hear my father: No, no, there is no need to die, it is not true that people die, it is we who are right, when I was coming back from the Causse Noir, the Causse Méjean, the Causse de Sauveterre, I might easily not have died—but for the whip, but for Indiana, but for the others, but for myself I would not have died—then Virginie, grave and gay: people must live, people must die— I can no longer distinguish my father's voice from Virginie's, I think however that it is he who is right, it is he who has the words, the pictures, in the darkness which falls and hides my book from me.

Glottones without depth.

34 Virginia 1542. 35 37.

44 Italian models estate on Virginia

Be